STERLING FIERCE AND
THE LIGHT WITCH

STERLING FIERCE AND THE LIGHT WITCH

STERLING FIERCE
BOOK TWO

LORI TCHEN

WISE WOLF
BOOKS

WISE WOLF BOOKS
An Imprint of Wolfpack Publishing
wisewolfbooks.com
701 S. Howard Ave. 106-324, Tampa, FL 33609

Cover design by Wise Wolf Books

Paperback ISBN 978-1-957548-88-3
eBook ISBN 978-1-957548-87-6
LCCN 2024932461

In memory of my dad, the original storyteller.

STERLING FIERCE AND THE LIGHT WITCH

CHAPTER ONE
RED SNOW

Sterling Fierce stood over the motionless body of a spiral-horned deer, uneasiness rippling in the pit of his stomach. The creature had been slain out in the open and discarded in the snow, uneaten by its killer—like the others. Sterling was a young hunter, sometimes rash in his decisions, but this wasn't his doing. He'd sworn to protect Everen, a duty he took very seriously. He was well-equipped with huntsman abilities beyond those of a full-grown hunter. As skilled as he had become, this was a dangerous quest that even a pack of seasoned hunters would have found challenging. Instead, the village elder, a wise and trusted Alin known for reading the future, had sent only Sterling. Everen had become tense and divided amid rumors of an impending Elvish war, and if the killer was a magic doer, more Everenians would turn their backs on the magic kind, flocking to join the efforts to ban the Elvish race.

Whatever the source, if magic was involved, Sterling was to keep it secret.

He believed these deaths were senseless but not without meaning. Someone or something was trying to send a message. Yet Sterling had tracked the string of carnage for days without getting any closer to finding answers. As he reassured the locals, his primary suspect was a rogue bear—possibly injured, starving, or rabid. In recent weeks, a black bear had been seen stalking then maiming local animals: a handful of horses, a dozen sheep, and one instance of a quarrel with a domesticated dog with wolf blood (likely the only reason it had survived the altercation at all). Villagers were spooked and superstitious, and they were quick to blame magic doers. Yet only a few of the folks Sterling had met had the courage to speak the truth as they saw it.

"Magic is at the root of these killings—dark magic, I can feel it in my bones," one villager from the eastern Bear Woods had reported after showing Sterling a blood-spattered henhouse full of scattered feathers and deep claw marks.

Along the borders of the Bear Woods, freshly nailed signs hung from trees.

Keep Out of Forests—Danger! one read.

And another warned *Beast on the Loose—Enter at Your Own Risk* in scrawled handwriting.

Once Sterling had reached the snow-covered base of the Artison Mountains, the signs had ceased. Along a rocky path that wrapped through the mountains, he'd met a wandering man with sunken eyes and a shaggy gray beard.

"The elves are to blame. They should leave Everen and take their war with 'em. Magic is unbalanced in our lands—two Elvish factions plotting against one another—nowhere is safe where powerful magic is weaponized," the man had opined.

Sterling shook off memories from the past few days and studied the slash marks across the deer's neck in front of him. A layer of winter fur had grown in perfectly, but that hadn't made a difference. The snow beneath the magnificent creature was stained a telltale red, and the attacker's clawed footprints trekked across the snowy landscape, the creature seemingly remorseless.

"Let's see if the beast left its mark," Sterling whispered.

He crouched close to the buck as his hunter senses activated, beginning with prickling in his ears. An unpleasant moaning came from the snow-tipped mountains above. Rock buried deep inside shifted ever so slightly, and besides Sterling, only a subspecies of cave bats had the ability to pick up the faint noise. Then, the nearby forest of pine trees released a pungent aroma that flooded his nose as he examined the deer's injuries with enhanced vision. An oily black residue darkened the slash marks. Sterling focused on it, his hunter's senses giving him more detail than any other hunter could have detected. His heart thumped, and his other unique ability, his blood magic, stirred as he sensed dark magic in the dark residue. Sterling's blood magic was designed to detect and kill witches. Combined with his hunter's senses, this made him what the old books referred to as a witch hunter.

The residue isn't from the natural world, Sterling discerned as a tingling sensation crept down the back of his neck. But as his pulse slowed, he recognized there wasn't a dark witch in the area either. He lifted the arctic fur mask from his face and itched his auburn mustache, smoothing out the bushier patches to cover the spots that hadn't grown in yet.

His gloved hand passed over the wide, clawed footprints and calculated the attacker's size and weight.

Bear tracks—a lone male as big as they come.

The arctic wind had already numbed his cheeks despite the rabbit fur mask Uncle Roag had made for him. The jolly mapmaker would have come along, but he was past his traveling years, slowed by a leg injury that had nearly taken his life. Sterling thought of his uncle, warm and comfortable in the village of Bren, probably gobbling down piping hot carrot stew and getting crumbs stuck in the curls of his ginger beard.

Sterling scooped snow with his travel-size spade and buried the mass of fur and horns in a shallow grave. It was the least he could do for the unfortunate creature. Tossing spadefuls of snow over the deer, Uncle Roag's warning from days ago echoed in his mind.

"The attacks don't add up. No meat's been eaten or so much as pecked at. Scavengers won't even touch it. I don't dare mention it to anyone, but this feels like before—the disease from the Dark Forest. Even though you destroyed Sellehn into a pile o' dust, another dark witch could've taken up her dirty work. Dark magic searches for those willing to do its bidding and pulls them away from the light. It gives them a taste of power and it never lets go. These attacks have everyone rattled, Nephew—even me. A beast roams the forests killin' and we don't know why. Hunter's word, it's not ordinary."

Sterling's mind reeled, trying to disentangle the mystery. He hadn't suspected magic at first, but now there was no denying it. But which magic doer was to blame? He hadn't detected a witch's presence, so he ruled out dark witches. Other suspects included goblins, rogue fairies, trolls, dark wizards, and dragons. Any number of magic beings could enchant a bear or shape-shift into one themselves. The villain could simply want to incite fear or panic—drive support away from the elves or try to run people from their land.

Days ago, the Alin had instructed Sterling, "Something is lashing out and leaving a trail of unfortunate creatures in its path, not to mention scaring our townspeople. They fear it will come to Bren next. Track the beast and stop it by whatever means necessary. Use your gifts. At fifteen years old, your abilities are already extraordinary, and they grow more powerful each day. Imagine what you can learn to do in the years to come—and there is no teacher like the wilds of Everen. You must protect this land and its people. As in times past, you may be one of the few who can."

It was a substantial responsibility—a heaviness that would've been trying for an adult who'd had a lifetime of experience. But the Alin was right. It was a witch hunter's duty to protect his homeland, as his father had done. Powerful blood magic flooded his veins. It could forge weapons more powerful (and terrifying) than anything humans could make. Even without a sword in hand, he was equipped to fight and destroy witches of the worst kind. He *was* a weapon, and he wanted to serve his purpose of fighting dark witches. But more than anything, Sterling wanted to earn the Fierce family name and live up to its reputation—he wanted to be an honorable hunter like his father had been. If war was indeed coming, he could get his chance to prove himself.

He closed the deer's eyes and said a hunter's prayer, scattering the last handfuls of snow over its curled horns.

CHAPTER TWO
TRACKING A KILLER

I cy wind blasted from the mountain peaks as Sterling tracked bear prints farther north. The large indentations wrapped around a mountain range so massive, it had split into three separate, full-sized mountains over the centuries. White specks swirled in every direction, which meant that a snow-storm was brewing. Soon everything, including the tracks, would be buried beneath a blanket of fresh snow. He had to hurry or risk losing the trail. He was close to the beast—he could feel it. At least for now, he had a bit of help.

I owe Uncle Roag a big favor for stitching together this ridiculous-looking mask for me. It's his most useful creation yet. Sterling fastened the fur tightly against his face. He squared his body toward the wind and sprinted with hunter speed until the hefty paw prints stopped abruptly near the edge of a pine tree thicket. A pocket of branches exposed tiny tufts of damp bear fur and freshly snapped branches. The damage was wide but short. After hours in the wind, the bear had finally opted for a sheltered path. It, too, must have felt a change in the weather, or perhaps it had caught the scent of a human close behind. Either way, Sterling was relieved to leave the chilling wind gusts and pelting snow behind.

Full, prickled branches swelled against his chest, neck, and head. The deeper he went, the more the pines resisted. Soon, he resorted to ducking until his back ached and his boots made sloshing sounds, full of melted snow.

The bear had an advantage traveling on all fours. That's not a bad idea, Sterling recognized, dropping to his knees as his enemy had. Pine needles poked and slapped against his head on the way down, and he wished the rest of his body were as numb as his toes.

Piney devils, he concluded.

Crawling on all fours helped, but it wasn't ideal. He envisioned his favorite reading spot at the end of his bed where the cotton blanket was worn to the threads but extra soft. He longed to be home and slurping piping hot potato soup while researching the Elvish race. Chasing a murderous bear in blizzard-like weather wasn't his idea of a favorable hunt, and besides, the real threat in Everen was an Elvish war. If he could turn around and go home, or think of one plausible excuse for doing so, he was sure he'd quit.

Just when the itching and stabbing grew to the point of nausea, the trees cleared away, and a wider path opened, flat and drenched in shadows. But that didn't bother Sterling. He'd traversed the infamous Dark Forest paths, comparable to walking in eternal nightfall. He shut his eyes and imagined returning to that place—he remembered its strange creatures and the smell of rotted tree fruit. When he opened his eyes, his night vision was active, instantly taking over as his primary sense, calming the others. His eyes glowed like bright gray storm clouds, sorting out shadowy shapes with ease. Seeing the world this way was to see it as other night creatures did. It was more serene, he thought, and he often preferred it.

The wind howled in the distance but didn't penetrate the thicket. Deep inside the pine forest, the air was quiet, an atmosphere perfect for hunting. Sterling weaved around a dirt path until the subtle trickle of water piqued his attention, and he followed it until he spotted a flowing, unfrozen river at least ten horse lengths wide. Before stepping from the cover of darkness, he instinctively set his hand on his dagger hilt.

Sterling shoved the fur mask off his face to rest on his windblown mop of curly, brown hair. He breathed in the refreshing scent of river water and mineral-rich mud. It was one of his favorite smells. The smooth river stones along the banks formed a familiar pattern. It reminded him of happier times when he'd gone camping as a boy with his father. Freshly caught fish would cook on the river stones laid over a hot fire while his father told stories.

Creatures of all kinds will come for a drink. It's a game

of patience and stealth, his father, the great hunter, Sir Rider Fierce, would've reminded him, had he been alive.

Sterling crept along the riverbank, scanning every detail without making a sound. Muddy bear tracks looped around, appearing on the other side of the bank. The paw indentations were the same width and depth as the ones he'd been following. And the lengthy claw marks matched the ones from the bloody henhouse and the animal carcasses trailing from the Bear Woods to the Artison Mountains.

This is the killer bear, Sterling realized as a familiar tingle tapped along his spine.

The beast had come here for a drink and would return to stalk other animals coming for the same reason. The bear wouldn't have gone far. This was, after all, the perfect hunting ground for a predator. Sterling's hearing alerted him to snapping limbs and shuffling in the bushes, so he ducked behind a tree to stay out of sight.

A pack of thirsty ring-tailed foxes lapped up river water before scurrying back into the forest. Next, an Arctic hawk swooped down, trapping fresh water in its beak before tossing its head back to swallow. And into the late evening hours, a cluster of stone-shelled frost snails as large as well-fed house cats (and twice a furry) came and went, leaving a trail of frozen crystal flurries and glittery slime behind.

Sterling fell into a state of relaxation as the hours droned past. He'd snacked on the last of his dried fish jerky and helped himself to fresh river water, before returning to his hiding spot. He began to doubt his plan. He didn't have the proper material to make a trap, which would do his job for him while he was away, and he had no way of calling the bear to him with an animal whistle or call horn. He had to trust his hunter's instinct and, as boring as it was, do nothing but wait.

As nightfall came, pockets of snow turned a majestic shade of purple. To hunters, snow was known as winter's jewel, able to bend light and sparkle, or glow in the darkness. Despite the beauty of the landscape, the temperature dropped too low. Sterling's heart rate slowed, making him less alert. His blood pulsed a three-beat pattern, a warning to find warmer shelter before falling into a hunter's hibernation in which he'd drift off into a deep sleep for days. But he didn't want to quit, not this close to finding the rogue bear. If only his body could stand the cold a little longer.

Snap.

The stench of musk barged into his nostrils, announcing the bear just before it came into view. Giant paws clumsily punched holes into the snow—it was massive, 1,300 pounds, Sterling gauged. The beast made its way to the stream and dipped its head down to drink. That was its mistake.

Sterling catapulted himself forward, aiming his dagger at the bear's heart. Despite the hunter's muffled approach and the creature's huge size, the bear had remarkably good reflexes. Meaty paws swiped at Sterling's head with astonishing accuracy. The young hunter was knocked flat on his back and sent rolling into the stream. His mask drowned somewhere out of sight. The frigid water pierced his clothing and stung his skin. Sterling struggled toward the surface but was knocked into the current as a huge body splashed in after him. He clung to his knife as a blur of muddy fur, bloodstained claws, and yellow teeth perfect for ripping into soft flesh appeared through the frosty water. Sterling forced himself upright, dodging bites and charges until he found himself wading into the deepest part of the river. He tucked in his head, took a gulp of air, and backflipped, disappearing beneath the racing river current. He'd have the advantage underwater, swimming with the flow and taking his scent with him.

Sterling swam beneath the water for as long as he could hold his breath. A good distance away, he made his way out of the river, straggling onto the muddy river's edge. There was no sign of the beast, so he returned his dagger to its sheath, then hunched over to catch his breath and removed his drenched shirt and cloak. He wrung them out and contemplated building a small fire, unsure of his next move.

Before his mind could settle, a giant bear paw burst from the water, swiping at Sterling's knees, knocking him facedown in the water. Sterling rolled to avoid another attack and scrambled across the icy river rocks. He snatched his clothing from the snow and skittered away as the bear roared a challenge. He prayed he could stay beyond the bear's reach and dashed toward a grove of trees, tossing on his shirt and cloak faster than ever. Loud splashing followed him. The bear pursued, undeterred, but by the grace of luck or destiny, the beast's paw got stuck in a mud hole.

Thank the forest spirits!

Sterling searched the forest for an escape route, but time was against him. The bear's sopping wet paw had sprung free. Sterling hoisted himself up the nearest tree, climbing several branches at a time, ascending nearly fifteen feet in the air. With wet boots and overpowering adrenaline, his foot slipped on a pinecone. Pine branches slapped him as he fell, and he nearly gagged when his cloak snagged on a branch, abruptly ending his freefall. Sterling clutched at the nearest branch and hoisted himself over it. He kicked, trying to find another branch to step on.

Hot breath tickled his ankle, and he jerked his legs upward.

The beast stood on its hind legs at the base of the tree, its head swiveling erratically. Then, Sterling locked eyes with the monster. Oily, black saliva dripped from its meat-shredding teeth. If only Sterling's blood magic could help, but his forearms didn't pulse hot the way they did when fighting a witch. He was on his own, and he knew it.

"You're bewitched, fella. You don't want to kill any more innocent animals—I'm just trying to help. Snap out of it! I don't want to hurt you, and you don't want to hurt me, right?" Sterling pleaded.

The bear hesitated for a moment before letting out a bellowing grunt and backtracking a few yards. The bear barreled toward the slender hunter piñata hanging from the tree branches.

"Oh no," Sterling sighed, squeezing the branch as tightly as he could.

His lungs heaved as cold air dried his throat. The bear slammed into the tree, knocking Sterling loose. Sterling flipped upside down and latched onto a tree limb with his legs. This time, he was within the bear's grasp, and a mouthful of teeth and black goo came at him. Sterling snatched up his dagger and stabbed deep into the bear's neck where a brightly lit symbol, a hunter's target, had appeared. Sterling's fatigued body plopped onto the soft, cold mud like a lifeless sack of pecans.

"It's time to go home where I can feel my toes again," Sterling said. He wrenched his dagger out of sticky fur as the bear's chest stopped rising. A close examination of the blackened blood on his dagger told him all he needed to know about the bewitched creature—this was the work of a witch.

Sterling dug a decent grave and said a hunter's prayer as he buried the giant beast.

"I'm sorry. You didn't deserve this, and I failed to save you. May you restore your peace in the afterlife where there is no more pain, no more loss—no more witches," he whispered. The last bit wasn't in the hunter's prayer, but he was sure his predecessors would understand, given the circumstances. "I mean, may you find eternal rest and harmony in the arms of the forest spirits."

He placed a sample of bear fur in his leather belt pouch and rubbed his arms. Ice had formed on the fabric of his sleeves, and he knew that if he didn't get warm, the cold would kill him as surely as a bear's paw. He scooped out a hollow in the snow, piling it up to make a short wall that blocked the wind. He lined it with pine branches on one side, then made a fire with the dry needles. Shivering, he hung as many clothes as he could spare over the hot flames, and he huddled back into the pine nest he'd made. Despite the calm that descended, he couldn't relax. The witch that had done this—she was out there, and she could do it again. He needed to leave at first light and get home. He needed answers, and his Alin was the only one who might have them.

Once most of the water had steamed out, he wrapped himself in his smoke-scented clothes. Then he banked the fire and prepared to rest, but a few hours into his light slumber, something made the hairs on his arms stand on end.

I'm not the only hunter here, he sensed, quickly activating his night vision and rising to a crouch so he could peer over his snow wall.

The weight of a huge animal slammed into his back, sending him face first through the snow and pine needles of his shelter. Knife-like talons pierced his clothing, stabbing his shoulder. He wrestled to get his arms underneath his body, but the creature was too heavy. He panted for breath and twisted his nose out of a snowbank. Sterling needed to know who'd hunted him—it wouldn't be an honorable hunter's death otherwise.

It was then that the snow leopard's distinct howl rang in his ears.

CHAPTER THREE
A TRUSTWORTHY VOICE?

The snow leopard's claws dug into the base of Sterling's head and neck. She stood firmly on his legs, pressing him into the cold snow like a giant boot squashing an ant. His right leg was bent under him at an awkward angle, and his face throbbed.

One of the arctic cat's paws lifted from his shoulder, and he had a fraction of a second to twist before her razor-sharp claws raked toward him. Her talons missed his spine and scraped through his cloak, the pointed tips snagging in tough threads. She shook her paw like a bewildered kitten.

If I can just get to my dagger...

He pressed his palms against the ground, trying to leverage his body up, but the cat hissed. Sterling froze, and she went back to shaking her entangled paw.

"I don't know if you can understand me," Sterling squeezed out words in short huffs. She paused to contemplate him in the light of his dying campfire. "I came through the White Mountains before—with a friend—a wizard. He told me you protect this land. I am no threat to you or your home."

The giant wildcat shook her front paw wildly, and the cloak's clasp dug into Sterling's throat. Sterling assessed his physical state—his ribcage would be badly bruised, but the mud and snow had cushioned him. *It is now or never*, he reasoned. Hunter's strength rushed through him, and as the cat tottered, still snagged in his cloak, he rolled onto his back, simultaneously undoing the clasp and tossing the fabric over the cat's thrashing body. She yowled as she stepped on the remains of the campfire and sprang into the air, the shredded cloak forgotten.

Sterling's hand was already on his dagger hilt. He tried to roll into a defensive crouch, but he had only gotten one leg under him when a blur of white fur was racing toward his face. Claws raked his forehead. Even with Sterling's enhanced reflexes, he couldn't avoid the cat's next attack. The full weight of her body slammed into his chest, knocking the wind out of him as he once again toppled to the ground. He wiggled his dagger hand free, but another paw knocked it loose. The silver-blue-tinted blade spun through the air with a metallic whistle. The cat's ears pricked, and her eyes flickered toward the gleaming edge of the knife for a mere moment.

Sterling head-butted the huntress in her furry rib cage, but she didn't budge an inch. Instead, her wild yellow-gray eyes lasered in on his pupils, and his eyes sparked with gray, glowing light. Her curiosity transformed into fear or anger, maybe both. Sterling gasped for breath, trying to remind his lungs how to function. The huge cat peered at him, assessing.

Her tail lashed across his feet, and Sterling snapped his boots together, catching the muscular tail. She whirled her head with a roar, her front paw leaving Sterling's chest.

Thank Everen's stars for feline reflexes.

Sterling pulled his knees to his chest and thrust his boots into the beast's belly. The cat reared onto her hind legs, and Sterling rolled to his feet, snatching his dagger as he rose.

The cat had to look up at him, but only just. She pulled back her lips and snarled.

"Good kitty..." Sterling whispered, trying to buy time as he carefully tested out his limbs to see if any had sustained breaks or sprains. No other words had come to mind, but even he knew it was a stupid thing to say.

The witch hunter locked eyes with the feral creature. She licked her lips, circling him. He was her prey, and she wanted him to know it.

Come on hunter's blood! Show me where to strike!

Sterling's mind scrambled, searching for a hunter's target to appear. This was usually how his magic worked. He'd delivered fatal blows to plenty of creatures (and witches). But this time, nothing happened. His hunter's instincts were pulling him in another direction. But that couldn't be. He blinked and tried to focus.

Then, he heard a girl's voice. A witch's voice, if the icy feeling in his throat was anything to judge by.

"Who's there?" He demanded, much less worried about the leopard and more concerned about the witch.

The snow leopard took advantage of his broken focus and leaped, razor-sharp claws aimed for the kill. Sterling's instincts returned enough to help him twist and avoid her paws, but he couldn't escape her teeth. Instead, he lifted his dagger as her wide mouth filled his vision.

But she never landed. The arctic wind stopped blowing, and the snow sparkled in the air. Bulging feline muscles and twitching fur hung motionless in the air, huge fangs inches from Sterling's throat. Leopard's breath brushed his cheek, but everything else was frozen. Sterling tried to take a deep breath, but he could barely gasp. He was frozen as well, his arm fixed with the dagger's point barely touching the soft white fur of the creature's chest. If they hadn't been frozen, they would both likely be dead.

Somehow, time had stopped, and neither he nor the leopard could move.

This is magic, but whose? he wondered. His hunter's blood pulsed as he struggled against his helpless position.

He tried to move his legs, but his toes gave no more than a wiggle, and his head swiveled only slightly before it stiffened more, as useless as a statue. Only his eyes were free to move about. It was the same for the leopard. Her gleaming yellow-gold eyes pierced through him, full of panic and confusion. Was this the witch's doing? If so, why had she frozen both of them rather than letting the snow leopard take out a helpless witch hunter?

Then, the girl's voice returned, forcing its way into his mind. His stomach knotted, convincing him that she could very well be a witch.

Please don't harm her. She is the protector of the Artison Mountains. This is her home. You would do the same to protect your homeland, hunter.

Sterling heard her words as clearly as he could understand wizard speak. He formulated a response.

If it's important, whoever you are, the snow cat attacked me first, not the other way around. I don't have a choice. I have to fight, Sterling said in his mind. This wasn't the kind of sentiment he'd expect from a witch. Perhaps she was some kind of forest spirit. She sounded more like a fairy, but his stomach had decided on a witch.

The girl raised her voice. *You always have a choice. You could have escaped. You chose to fight instead. You rely too strongly on your magic. If you harm her, this land will lose its only guardian and put Everen in imbalance. You should know more than anyone what that means, Sterling Fierce.*

Sterling closed his eyes, and his dagger's glow dimmed. It was true. He'd only asked his hunter's magic how to fight the beast, not how to escape. But he wasn't sure if he should trust this strange voice that mysteriously knew his name. His mind reeled, thinking of magical beings he'd met. He didn't recognize this voice at all.

Who are you? he asked.

If you choose the right path, you will live to find out, her voice shook slightly. *Choose quickly! Time is persistent, and this spell will not hold much longer.*

He took one more look into the leopard's eyes before closing his own. He knew what he had to do.

Hunter's blood, show me safety. Show me an escape path.

Tiny specks of light spun out from his wrists and popped on and off. Glowing blue swirls and spheres appeared in the snow, swirling toward the river. But it wasn't enough; the snow leopard was too close. If time unfroze, even if he missed stabbing her in the heart, he'd never get to the river before she tore him apart.

I can't outrun her, not in the snow, he explained to the mysterious voice.

I will keep her frozen as long as I can. Go now!

Something in the girl's voice was desperate, even afraid. He didn't know why, but he trusted her. The rogue bear was dead, after all. His task here was done, and he wanted more than anything to return home.

Release me now, he said to the girl before taking one last gulp of air.

CHAPTER FOUR
STORYTELLING

"Well, your story explains how you got those nasty scratches on your face! And what happened to your cloak. But then what? You rolled into the freezin' cold stream and it whisked ya away? The snow cat didn't try to follow?" Uncle Roag's unkempt eyebrows rose high like bushy red squirrel tails peeking over a tree branch. He leaned forward eagerly. Sterling shook his head.

"That's exactly it. I floated away, then came home."

Sterling sat in his uncle's creature-filled home, curled up in his favorite chair. The arms were crafted from wood so old and worn, it felt like fine leather against the palms of his hands. Being here should have soothed him, but instead, the girl's voice played in his mind, as if she were still calling to him. He hadn't thought about her during his trek home, thankful to be alive and unfrozen (in both ways). Hunting, tracking, and fighting had drained him, but his blood magic had gone untapped lately, and it grew restless the longer he went without slaying a witch. He could return to the mountains and find the girl— the witch—and satisfy his blood's stored up energy. But she seemed different from the dark witches he'd fought before—he didn't necessarily *want* to destroy her. It was a mystery that he'd have to solve, even if it meant going to the Artison Mountains again.

Uncle Roag had busied himself in the kitchen, pouring heaps of potato stew into a blue-speckled bowl designed to mimic a land bird from an island nobody else had heard of.

"Good news is the killings have stopped. And that's all because of you! Villagers don't talk of magic doers and curses and dark magic. A rabid bear does exactly what this one did—mystery solved. My brave hunter—you did good, Nephew," he said, whistling an old hunter victory tune.

"Thanks," Sterling muttered. His uncle asked a few more questions, but Sterling drifted into his head again.

There was something out there—dark magic residue in the wilds of Everen, and Sterling had felt it. Despite the great protector, the Red Wolf, returning to the Vionin Kingdom recently, Everen wasn't safe with the impending Elvish war. Sterling wondered about his wolf friend and if he, too, and other magic creatures had sensed the darkness. Its faint pulse tapped against his skin like vibrations of ocean waves that had weakened on their journey. But at their source, something stronger brewed. He hoped the dark energy would stay tucked away in isolated bits, too weak to threaten more than a rogue toad or lost elk unfortunate enough to cross its path. But only a fool would believe Everen would be without enemies for long.

"Ahem," Uncle Roag bellowed, tugging logs into the stone hearth. "...it's like this ol' stone hearth I built with my own hands. She's painted with black soot but strong as a fortress."

"Yes, Uncle," Sterling said with a nod before burying his confused expression behind a mug of spice tea. He hadn't been listening, but for the first time in days, his mind was free to wander without having to be on high alert. He couldn't stop it even if he wanted to.

Who was the girl, and why was she desperate to save the snow leopard? Why even bother helping me escape? And how did she know my name?

Fire crackled and popped in a familiar melody. Doddel birds pecked at a mess of scattered seeds on the windowsill, their bright orange beaks clacking against the wood.

Thump.

A chunk of half-eaten cornbread plunked him square between his stormy gray eyes, interrupting their intense, swirl motion.

"Talkin' to you, silly boy! Did ya freeze your ears off up there in them mountains?" Uncle Roag belched loudly enough to spook the poor doddel birds from the window. Seeds scattered onto wooden floor planks; their plunks disguised by furious flapping sounds.

Sterling sighed, releasing the last of the arctic air from his lungs. He felt the chill from the North finally leave his body, but he wouldn't soon forget the cold that had dogged his journey.

"You always had a solid aim, Uncle, even if you've traded arrows for slobbery bread," Sterling said with a grin.

"I don't get'ta adventure much farther than my garden these days, lad. Not with my bad leg and all. Come on, don't keep a good story to yourself!"

Uncle Roag shoved a heaping spoonful of potato stew into his mouth. Dense brown droplets dripped onto his bright red beard, joining a host of cornbread crumbs and leftover food from meals past.

Squirrel-tail brows rose again, and Uncle Roag's green eyes gleamed like unearthed emeralds soaking in sunshine.

Sterling swirled a heavy metal spoon in his mug of stew. Steam curled into the air as if an invisible string beckoned it.

"The river saved me but gave me a good lashing along the way. I bumped and scraped against every rock and boulder like I'd been garbled up inside an ice giant's mouth. My legs and arms went numb as the current picked up speed, but I didn't mind that bit—didn't have to feel any pain. My arms glued to my side like Father taught me, I shot southward—

imagined I was an arrow flying faster and faster. When the current finally slowed, I crawled out and thanked Everen's stars for grass and dirt instead of endless snow. I called for Banefield. That whistle worked like a charm." Sterling pulled a small wooden tube out of his pocket. It could produce a sound that carried over long distances, but it was pitched so that only a horse (or someone with hunter's blood) could hear it. "He found me in record time. Smartest horse, I tell you." Sterling slurped his stew and relished the warmth filling his belly.

"You're lucky the leopard didn't jump in after ya! How'd you know you could make it?" Uncle Roag pried.

The girl's voice. Sterling knew it was best not to mention it. Disembodied voices made people feel uneasy, and he didn't want to ruin a happy story or a pleasant evening.

"Instinct, I suppose. Like how Banefield knew where to find me." Sterling changed the topic and hoped his uncle wouldn't press for more.

"Ah, the worth of a wizard's horse! The elders say Rarick horses are more valuable than their weight in gold. Aye, why do you think the wizards ride them? They bond with their riders, always know where they are, in this life and the next," Uncle Roag said with a wink. "The only beast more loyal is an Acreedian dragon. Your grandfather had a bond with one, and even though he's gone, may he rest in peace, that old dragon won't have forgotten the Fierce blood, and don't you forget it."

"I won't forget, Uncle," Sterling said patiently, but once Roag got started, there wasn't any point in interrupting his story, so Sterling settled in to listen to an epic tale of a young hunter and an Elvish dragon.

That night, Uncle Roag hummed an old song that mapmakers sang when they'd finished their work. Sterling could finally relax, buried beneath quilted blankets and breathing in the scent of map paper and ink-filled bottles. In the moonless night, clouds swept by as if they had somewhere important to be. Perhaps there was another force, just as real, that carried the girl's voice to him in the mountains, and maybe it wasn't evil. Whatever kind of witch she was, she was powerful. But because of her, he was alive. Sterling needed answers, and there was only one person who might have them.

CHAPTER FIVE
THE VOICE

Wind rattled the crisp autumn leaves of the hillside trees as morning sunshine flickered from behind scudding clouds. Sterling led Banefield up the solitary path to the Alin's cottage on the outermost edge of the village. Few knew how to find the Alin, and fewer had the courage to approach his home. The narrow path was riddled with loose rocks and shrouded in shadows. The trees grew crooked from the roots up, and the limbs were bent in odd places. The way they stuck out in all directions was unnatural, like they'd been struck by dark lightning, as his father would have said (but that was probably made up). Sterling thought they looked like wooden statues of lightning fairies that had met their deaths in a terrible circumstance. This would've been disturbing, but Sterling had been traveling this path since he was small, and he'd long since gotten over any trepidation.

"Well, nothing's changed, huh ol' boy?" Sterling asked his horse as he took greater strides up the path. "C'mon, keep up."

Banefield replied with a snort, intentionally slowing as his hoof skittered on the rocky path.

The air smelled like charred oak moss and mushroom mold. "The Alin lives like a recluse up here. But I can't blame him. I'd prefer the trees over the villagers' gossip too."

Despite their blackened branches, the trees sprouted a myriad of brightly colored leaves. The same sense of wonder washed over him as it had when he was a child.

The Alin's magic must have warped these trees, he'd decided.

Traveling this path as a boy, it had always been secret business and hushed conversations. It was out here he'd learned that powerful magic could live in ordinary things, like trees. Sometimes, he swore he heard voices when the branches creaked—whispers in the wind. But they were always in a foreign language —none that he'd heard before or since. Maybe it was his imagination. Maybe it was magic.

Banefield grunted as more rocks dislodged beneath his hooves.

"I know it's a hike, but we're almost there," Sterling said. "I bet you miss your flying enchantment. I'm sorry it stopped working, buddy. We'll figure out how to recharge it soon."

They trekked along the last slanted bit until the

hilltop spilled into meadows of emerald grass like a calm green ocean.

"Go snack on as much grass as you want, Banefield. The Alin will be glad to see you."

Sterling released a deep breath and shook off the nerves that had crept into the base of his throat—the same ones that started up the moment he'd returned to Bren. The girl from the mountains weighed on his thoughts again. She was powerful enough to speak into his mind without being near him. She could stop time, at least temporarily, but that was a rare ability—something even the Alin could not do.

Sterling knocked on the thick wooden door with two loud knocks followed by two slow knocks, then four rapid taps (the secret code). Silence followed. Sterling used his enhanced hearing to listen inside, but there was no rummaging of books or fresh aroma of pipe smoke.

A faint clinking sound emerged from above.

Sterling squinted toward the darkening clouds where the clinking was loudest. Blackbirds with slick feathers flew in perfect V formation. Their legs dangled with tiny metal trinkets, the telltale sign of their master.

"The Alin will be home soon. His birds are returning ahead of him," Sterling explained, but Banefield had made his way into the meadow, chomping away happily.

Sterling smiled at his loyal horse and sat on the porch. He didn't mind waiting here. It was serene, comprised of nature instead of people, which Sterling preferred. It was far from noisy townsfolk and judgmental stares. The crowded market would be saturated with sellers, buyers, and deafening chatter this time of morning.

Sterling retrieved a horse brush from the shed. It hung from the same rusty nail as always, between a cobweb and other horse tools. He brushed Banefield's silky silver-white coat and let his mind drift.

"I'd be crazy to go back to those mountains, Banefield. The snow leopard knows my scent now. If she sniffs a bead of my sweat anywhere near her territory, she'll hunt me down with vengeance. But...I still want to go back," he admitted.

The brush's rounded metal teeth collected shiny metallic locks into a matted swirl. Usually, the repetitive motion of brushing the massive animal and the scent of horse dust soothed Sterling. But a knot of worry tugged from the pit of his stomach—it was the kind that refused to be ignored. It would soon crawl into his throat until he couldn't push it away any longer.

That girl's voice means something. I need to know who she is, he decided.

The brush went still. Banefield shifted his weight from one leg to the other and nuzzled the distracted witch hunter.

"You always know when I have a secret, buddy," Sterling confessed as his eyes scanned the horizon. "Alright, I'll tell you. In the White Mountains, I met a girl—well, not in person. She was just a voice. Maybe a snow spirit or something. She protected the snow leopard. She froze time—at least for a few moments. She let me escape if I promised to leave the snow leopard unharmed."

Banefield picked his front hoof up and stomped the grass.

"Yeah, you heard right. She froze time! I've never seen anyone, not even a wizard, do that," Sterling whispered, unable to hide how impressed he felt.

Just then, a tap echoed against the rocky soil in the distance. Sterling zeroed in on a hooded figure—a man with a long, silver beard and a glossy staff that Sterling would recognize anywhere. The fine blue silk robe he wore had intricate designs of stars, moons, and suns sewn with exquisite skill and golden thread.

Sterling beamed at the sound of the Alin's metal beard trinkets clinking together softly as he marched toward the hut.

"Sterling, it is good to see you have returned safely. The fresh battle scars will be favored by the village girls—a daring hunter who rid the forest of a dangerous predator," the Alin said in a pleasant tone. "You did well. Every day, you are closer to growing a formidable beard to be adorned with trinkets of your own—fairies, wood sprites, and princesses will gift you with trinkets of your own when you complete quests for them. Now, to what do I owe this visit?" he inquired with a welcoming smile.

Sterling stroked his short, auburn mustache as his

gray eyes swirled with a storm of questions inside, ready to burst out.

"Tomorak, something strange happened in the White Mountains," Sterling replied in a voice more like his father's than his own.

Abruptly, the wind blew from the east instead of the north, and storm clouds marched in. The Alin brushed his beard, twisting some of the trinkets before tucking the longer part of his beard into his robe.

"Is this to do with the wild bear, the snow leopard, or the witch?" the Alin queried without hesitation.

Sterling's jaw plopped open. His head went fuzzy, and his stomach hardened into a cold ball.

"I knew she was a witch—but how did you?" he sputtered. "She was just a girl—her voice was soft and kind."

"Not all witches are old and hideous. The girl is a light witch. She practices helpful enchantments and studies magic for educational purposes. She is about your age, I'd say. Her name is Evenna."

A light rain began but the sky darkened, threatening to downpour any moment. Banefield took cover beneath a large, crooked tree. Sterling pulled his hood over his head as he and the Alin hurried to the cottage.

"How do you know about her?" Sterling gasped, ducking under a split board that jutted out from the front porch.

The Alin aimed his staff at his front door handle,

and it began to glow with white light. The door opened, and the Alin turned toward Sterling.

"I should know all about her. Evenna is my granddaughter, and I believe you will soon meet her properly," he whispered, flashing a delighted smile.

CHAPTER SIX

THE CARETAKER'S CHOICE

The news pulsed through Sterling's blood. His stomach hardened with a familiar stone-cold sensation.

"With all due respect, sir, my blood magic was made to destroy witches. I can't go anywhere near her," Sterling said flatly. He paced back and forth inside the Alin's cottage, the floorboards creaking with each footfall.

"Sterling, the relationship between witches and witch hunters is not fully understood. You know that. Dark witches—they threaten peace and all that is good, and your blood magic targets them as the threats that they are, but light witches are unlike their infamous cousins. I believe it would be wise to explore the other side of witches. As the only living witch hunter, it is your responsibility to try and understand that relationship," the Alin advocated.

Stumped, Sterling turned and rested his forehead

against the glass pane of a round window. He huffed hot breath onto the glass and dragged his finger through it, forming a question mark.

"Are we capable of not destroying each other?"

The Alin's aged face wore the same amused grin as before. "Maybe you are the best person to answer that question." He chuckled softly as he brewed a kettle of hot wormwood tea (no worms this time) and enchanted a floating wooden waterfall. The pieces made clunking and clopping sounds as they formed and reformed while hovering in the air.

Sterling hated advice that came in the form of a puzzle, and it displeased him that the Alin handled the matter so lightly. Still, the thought of seeing the light witch tempted him.

"I am to find her. Learn from her—about light witches and their magic. My next quest is to find peace between them and, well, me. Right?" Sterling asked, holding back a healthy dose of panic and an ounce of pride. For once, he may have been a step ahead of the Alin.

The wooden waterfall poured steamed milk into a mug of hot water.

"Have some tea," the Alin said as the mug slid toward him across the knotty, misshapen table. Sterling obliged, taking his seat with a thud.

The mug stopped precisely in front of Sterling's hand. Painted violet butterflies wisped across the ceramic cup. Two large eyes emerged, then delicate eyelashes sprung outward and fluttered at him.

Magic can be so distracting.

Sterling scooted his chair away, pacing the length of the table. Like a puppy, the magical mug floated near his hand until he felt obligated to hold it. The lashes tickled his hand as he picked it up, but the delicious wormwood tea with a woodsy, burnt cream flavor was soothing.

The Alin retired to his usual quilted chair in the corner where the shadows were darkest.

"My young hunter, your next quest is to save her. I have reason to believe she reached out to you for help. She got your attention—and mine—for a reason. She is very special. All the more reason she belongs here, where she can grow her powers without fearing them," the Alin said, sipping from his own enchanted mug. Petite silver animations resembling stars and planets orbited around the mug's surface.

"Save her," Sterling repeated the words, but they were drowned with doubt. "I'm sorry. I—I'm the wrong person. I'm a witch *hunter*. What happens if my blood attacks her and I can't stop it?"

"You are precisely the one to do it. You are inherently programmed to track witches—are you not? You can find Evenna faster than anyone—and you may be the only one who can. I need you to bring her to me so I can keep her safe. Think of it as a catch-and-release exercise, you know, like fishing," the Alin said in a calm tone. He spoke as if he were reassuring a chef making a new dish instead of a hunter being asked to work against his own instincts.

"Keep *her* safe? She may be young, but she's plenty powerful. What does she need saving from?" Sterling asked bluntly.

"From the elder witches who were supposed to care for her and teach her light magic. Evenna's magic grew too powerful, and the spineless old grouches locked her away. Evenna is alone and scared, Sterling. Witches, no matter how pure of heart, should not be isolated. If she does not escape, her powers will become corrupted—she will undoubtedly turn to dark magic. I tried to tell the elders, but having never raised a young witch, they are out of their depth. We had a terrible fight, and they've moved her—hidden her from me. The protection spell is from the old texts—simple enough but highly effective—it keeps me out. And now, I fear Evenna's light is fading. You see, you must be the one to find her for me. I just hope we are not too late," the Alin whispered, blowing steam from the top of his mug.

"So, I need to break into the witches' hut, rescue your granddaughter—who happens to be a powerful light witch—hope that we don't destroy each other, and flee across Everen with very angry elder witches chasing after us. Am I missing anything?" Sterling panted as he spoke. His throat was as dry as sandpaper. He chugged the rest of his tea and stood with his hands on his hips like he would when pouting to his father.

"You mustn't forget that Evenna hasn't seen much of Everen outside of what her caretakers have allowed. You will need to teach her along the way," the Alin continued, ignoring Sterling's sarcasm.

"This is impossible," Sterling sighed.

"Nothing is impossible. You will learn to control your blood, Sterling—do not let it control you."

Sterling closed his eyes and searched for the right words. This couldn't be as simple as the Alin was making it out to be.

"Evenna and I are natural enemies. It's in our blood. There is no controlling that. Is there?"

The Alin shuffled over to an off-kilter shelf that leaned over at such an angle that the books appeared to be floating in place. He took his time perusing the makeshift library before selecting a book with a creased black leather cover, then returned to his corner chair. The title was printed in bold copper lettering, some deviation of an ancient language. Pages turned, and the Alin was silent as he read and puffed on his pipe.

"Look, hunter, peaceful witches—light witches. Are *they* your enemy?" he asked, holding the book open. He pointed at a sketch of a being resembling a snow fairy high in the mountains. There was another drawing on the next page—a child riding an albino cat.

No. Maybe, he contemplated. "I don't know. You never know with the magic kind," Sterling rebutted with a scowl.

"You ARE the magic kind, boy!" the Alin boomed, waving his hands, dimming all the candles at once.

Sterling jumped back a step, eyes darting toward the back door in case he needed to make a run for it.

A mist crept into the room, and the air grew frigid. The Alin drew a spindly wand from his robe pocket, and the celestial symbols on his cape glowed. Lilac smoke circled Sterling then etched a girl's face into the air. Her wide-set eyes appeared panicked. Her face was round with full cheeks. Swoops of thick hair swept across her chin, drawing attention to a star-shaped pendant resting snugly against her neck.

"My young white witch," he said, beaming with pride. "When she spoke to you in the mountains, did you wish to harm her?"

"No," Sterling said without pause but keeping his back against the wall and his eye on the door.

"And now, when you see her face, do you wish to destroy her?"

"No," Sterling repeated, acutely aware of the witch's beauty. *Appearances don't always matter*, he reminded himself as his shoulders relaxed. "But a voice and a magical portrait are not real. What if my blood attacks her as soon as I get near her? I've killed every witch I've ever met, without hesitation. When my blood takes over, there's no stopping it."

"Your blood did what you willed it to do—what you needed it to do. If you don't *want* to harm Evenna, teach your blood to obey. You can control your abilities," he explained. He relit his pipe and blew smoky spheres into the air. They danced around and through Evenna's spirit-like portrait. The witch and her worried expression and starry necklace faded, leaving only white sparkles behind.

The candle flames popped back up to full strength, warming the room, and the mist trickled into the floorboards, out of sight.

Sterling recalled the crowded marketplace in his village. He couldn't even control his wandering instincts to focus on the tasks before him when he was among nonmagic humans. How was he going to command ancient blood magic while in close quarters with a powerful witch?

"I'm sorry, but I am not ready for a quest like this," Sterling confided, looking intently out the window at Banefield, who was still grazing the meadow. The rain had calmed, but Sterling felt more anxious now than before. He wanted to help Evenna, but he wouldn't be able to forgive himself if he destroyed her.

"What if I tracked her, and you came with me?" Sterling asked.

"I wish that I could be the one to save her, but the elders are keeping tabs on me—if they noticed me approaching, they'd move Evenna somewhere else before I could come close," the Alin moped. "And then there's the trouble with a new monster—don't worry, I won't make you kill this one. He's been following me after I went—well, never mind. The monster is a *hobbelston*—as nasty as they come, but he only attacks at night. I am holding a protection spell during the nighttime, so he doesn't interfere with the townspeople. But I must be here to do it.

"As Evenna's rightful caretaker, I will choose her rescuer. And I choose you, Sterling Fierce. Your uncle prepared a map that will take you to the last place I sensed her energy. It is a far journey, I'm afraid—to the Ice Lands," he said with finality.

Sterling locked eyes with the Alin. This was an order, and he could not refuse—not if he wanted a home in Bren—and not if he didn't want to bring shame upon the Fierce family name.

"I have one request if you'll allow it," Sterling replied.

"Whatever you need."

"Premadora comes with me," he insisted.

"Ah, the plendi. She's rather a good luck charm for you, isn't she? I'm afraid she has other duties that must be attended to, but she may accompany you to the edge of the Great River—no farther. Prepare to leave at first light. And do not destroy my grand-daughter, Sterling Fierce," the Alin said.

This time he didn't grin.

CHAPTER SEVEN
A PLENDI'S WARNING

Coaxing Premadora out of her enchanted box was an ordeal even the Alin didn't bother with. If he woke her before her energy was restored, she would be more cross than usual. But delaying Sterling's journey was not an option. So the Alin sprinkled sleeping dust over Premadora's shimmery eyelids and whisked her into a petite riding satchel on Banefield. Pointy-tipped wings twitched as her tiny half fairy, half plant body slid into the leather pouch.

"She'll be safe and snug atop Banefield. You must travel quietly but swiftly, Sterling. She will wake up soon. I hope she proves helpful to you, but she has important work here. Before you reach the Great River Bridge, she must return to me," he whispered. "I am afraid that is all the time I can spare her for."

Sterling didn't have time to wonder what secret business Premadora and the Alin were up to. In his experience, when magic was needed in a hurry, it never meant that anything good was happening. He pushed his curiosity aside and rode to his Uncle Roag's cottage. They exchanged hushed farewells, making sure to avoid waking the sleeping plendi. Although this was not their first goodbye, Sterling always found it hard to leave his uncle behind. He was the only family Sterling had left. And the white hairs growing in his beard, just as burly and curly as the fiery red ones, were the subtle yet definite markings of old age settling in.

But this morning, Uncle Roag was as boisterous and quick-witted as ever, and he made Sterling promise to be safe and wise on his travels (a promise that had become their tradition before every quest).

With his uncle's map in hand and his good luck charm snoring on a pillow of glitter, Sterling patted Banefield's shoulder and steered him east.

As they cleared the outskirts of Bren, Premadora's satchel twitched.

"Why in Everen do I smell horsehair and human?!" Premadora screeched. "I don't like it—not at all!"

Banefield gave a soft neigh, but that didn't calm down the irate plendi. Premadora shot out of the satchel and fluttered her wings into a frenzy.

"Easy, now, Premadora. You could act a little cheerful to see me and Banefield," Sterling said. He couldn't hold back a hearty smile. "After all, we're glad to see you. It's been a long time since our last adventure together."

Her cheeks flushed a rosy hue and bright green plant stem arms crossed snugly over her chest.

"Hmph!"

Premadora whizzed into the sky and complained in fairy speak. A trail of telltale sparkles chased her from cloud to cloud. Sterling bit his lip to keep from laughing out loud.

"Don't worry, buddy, she'll be back. You remember she's a tad temperamental, but it's all part of her charm," Sterling said with a chuckle as he scratched Banefield's neck. "C'mon let's get moving. She'll catch up."

Soon, they reached the golden wheat fields beyond Bren's borders. Sterling startled as a puff of glitter exploded on his nose. Premadora floated to her favorite resting spot in between Banefield's ears and released a high-pitched yawn.

"So, tell me what all this is about, Mr. Big Fancy Hunter," she bossed.

"I was starting to worry that you didn't want to join us," Sterling said with a comical pout.

"I'm not fond of being kidnapped. But I suppose there's a good reason the Alin allowed this thievery, especially with all the work I've to do," Premadora spouted.

"Yes, he mentioned your work. What was it again? Top secret fairy business?" Sterling snooped.

"Oh, never mind that. Tell me, boy, where are we going, and why have you summoned me?" She picked cloud mist out of her wings, preoccupied.

Sterling smiled. Premadora was the only one who still called him "boy," but she said it with endearment (and sarcasm).

He sighed. "The truth is, I need your help. The Alin will only let you stay until we reach the Great River, so we don't have long. I'm supposed to rescue his granddaughter from some elder witches. Evenna, his granddaughter, that's her name. I am to deliver her to Bren, to the Alin, unharmed."

"Rescuing a lovely maiden is not such a troubling quest for a brave hunter such as yourself. Why do you...What are you hiding?" Premadora asked, swiping her thick silver-streaked hair over her shoulder, and tucking it behind one wing. She glared at him suspiciously.

"Well, uh, Evenna is sort of a powerful girl—um, witch—a light witch—a good witch, I suppose. That's why the elders locked her away, hidden from the Alin, or else he'd be the one going after her. I think they're scared of her powers."

Premadora's eyes glowed a pale teal and sparkles dripped from her lashes as she blinked.

"Tell me, what memories do you have of your childhood—before your father brought you to Bren?"

"Premadora, I'm not sure how that is helpful, and we don't have time to—" Sterling began.

"Answer the question or I'll fly back home this instant!"

Premadora's wings buzzed. She was dead serious.

"Um, going hunting with my dad—normal hunting stuff."

"No, you can do better. Tell me the earliest childhood memory—the first one that pops into that messy-haired head of yours," Premadora snapped.

"Campfires and snowfall and meat roasting over golden flames. There were purple-barked trees that glowed in the dark and glittery trails of dust in the sky. Sometimes I think it was a dream and not a memory at all," Sterling admitted, relieved to talk about the image that had floated in his mind all these years.

"You have described the ancient forests of the Northern Ice Lands. Though the trees are white-barked—not purple. The snow reflection muddles colors. You must have stayed there for a time, as a child. But it's not a safe place for a witch hunter, for it is also home to the light witches. They are few, but they are powerful," Premadora explained.

"I've never met a light witch before," Sterling said. "But aren't they, you know, good? This girl—I need to know how to be around her and not attack her. My blood magic is not exactly ready to be tamed, and I can't risk hurting Evenna."

"Light or dark, good or bad, witches, especially powerful ones, will trigger your instincts. You were born to hunt witches, and your blood magic is destined to destroy them," Premadora warned.

"But the Alin said I could control my instincts—that my blood would listen to me. He said if I didn't want to harm Evenna, I wouldn't. You've always told me the truth, no matter how awful it was. Do you believe I will harm her?" Sterling asked.

"The Alin is wise, and he knows of magic history— he must know of chapters that I do not," she conceded, turning her gaze to the path ahead.

They approached the Great River Bridge, and Premadora's wings dimmed, and the sparkles in her eyes darkened. "I will tell you the truth as I know it— but I do not wish to disrespect the Alin."

Sterling nodded, signaling that he would keep her words secret.

"Your blood magic is strong. It will desire to destroy Evenna. The longer you resist, the more likely your blood will turn against you. It is said that a witch hunter's blood can reverse in the veins, turning cold. It is you, Sterling Fierce, who is in danger."

CHAPTER EIGHT
BLUE LIGHTNING

Lornia was the most established village along the Great River. There was plenty of green meadow grass for Banefield to eat, the perfect place for a brief rest before crossing the Great River. Besides, the village was a sight to see. Giant stones stood in a massive circular border surrounding the peaceful community of fishermen and craftsmen. Normally, Sterling felt a sense of wonder being near the ancient stones, but today he aimed at not vomiting. Premadora shifted nervously as Sterling swung out of the saddle and sat on the grass.

"How does the Alin not know about this?" Sterling asked, bewildered at the Alin's lack of sight. His blood pulsed harder, and his temples ached.

"The Alin is desperate to save his granddaughter— blinded by love. Besides, he is wise, but witch hunters are rare—you cannot expect him to know everything about your kind. He cannot act as your father," Premadora whispered, landing on his knee.

Sterling's eyes flashed, filled with bolts of gray lightning.

"Yes, I remember my father is dead," he snarled.

"I just meant that the Alin is not an expert on witch hunters. There are few who are. He'll understand if you explain the danger you'd be in if you went. This is not your quest," Premadora declared. "I've told you all I can. Now, I must return to Bren—I have certain urgent business to attend to," she said in her usual bossy tone as her wings zipped into the air. "I suspect I'll see you again soon?"

"Premadora, wait."

He dusted sparkles out of his eyes and shook off memories of his father. "I can't let Evenna stay locked away—she's his family. I know what it's like to lose family. Besides, she'll go dark and then I'll really have no choice but to destroy her. There must be something I can do. What are the rules? How long can I be near her before my blood, you know, tries to kill her, or turns against me?"

"You should know by now that magic makes its own rules," Premadora uttered, looking back toward Bren, furrowing her brow. "I really don't have time."

"Please. I need your advice." Sterling swallowed hard. "And wisdom."

Premadora gave her best told-you-so teacher smile, lowering her wings. "How I adore flattery. Oh, Everen's great seas, I'll share the last bit I can pull from my memory. Some of this, what I'm about to tell you, is based on rumor, passed to me from the fairies —but it is truly all I can tell you, Sterling."

She closed her eyes as her entire body pulsed with glowing teal light as she seemed to unlock another part of herself. The world around them fell silent except for the sound of Premadora's small, high-pitched voice.

"If Evenna is to be saved, she can only be tracked by a witch hunter. Sterling Fierce, you are the only one who can save her, but it is your choice if you wish to continue your quest. Once your blood senses her, time is against you. Your blood will try to fight her. If you resist, your blood will go into shock, confused—fighting against its very nature. It will reverse flow, and you will be in danger beyond measure. No one can say when—hours, maybe days. The reversed blood will go cold. When that happens, you will have no choice but to destroy the witch. Or your blood will destroy you."

A bright light flashed from her body as she opened her eyes and returned to normal. Her words of warning echoed in his mind. Her wings perked up and pointed toward Bren.

"Thank you, Premadora," he said with a shaky smile.

"Save Evenna if you can. But save yourself too. Oh, and go around the kingdom, not through it this time!" Premadora said before disappearing, leaving behind only a puff of glitter.

"Why is that important?" he asked, but it was no use.

A trail of sparkles zipped along the trail and disappeared. Sterling took a deep breath and rose to his feet. He unrolled Uncle Roag's map, which highlighted a new path between the Dark Forest and the Swamplands that would take him closer to Evenna. The venomous swamp flies kept to their mossy green watery home during the daytime but ventured out after nightfall. Uncle Roag had enchanted the map to reveal swarms of vile insects and their movements. Black wiggling lines on the parchment were a warning not to be taken lightly. If Sterling was to reach the safety of the Vionin Kingdom roads, he'd need to skirt north of them. He climbed into his saddle and nodded to Banefield.

"I need your speed, buddy. Do your enchanted horseshoes still ride over water?" Sterling asked his horse.

Banefield stomped his front right hoof and released a deep snort, angling his massive body toward the Great River Bridge.

"Then we ride!" Sterling exclaimed, squeezing his heels against Banefield's sides.

This time of year, the mountain air breathed down from the snow-tipped landscape in the not-so-far distance. Daylight had faded into a moonless night before Banefield's hooves touched the Vionin Kingdom roads. They stopped for a short rest, keeping a lookout for wondering swamp flies, then pressed on into the wee hours of morning.

Frigid wind whispered through Sterling's loose clothing, tossing his bearskin cape from side to side as the darkness crept in. Had it not been for the enchanted Vionin Kingdom roads' natural glow, the journey would have halted until morning—too dark and cold to carry on. He sniffed. His favorite cloak had been lost during the fight with the snow leopard, and this was an old cape of his uncle's. It smelled much worse than his previous one.

"We can make it to the kingdom soon and rest at the base of the mountains," Sterling said, tightening the reins. "The wind will be less sharp there," he said as a shiver spread across his back, chilling his sweat into icy droplets.

Sterling steered Banefield along the shimmering path, the glowing stones as their guide. They twinkled as if they contained bits of distant stars—perhaps they did. Sterling pretended they were winking at him from below the horse hooves, which helped pass the time. Despite the distraction, he struggled to keep his eyes open.

"I wish Premadora could've stayed longer," he confessed.

Banefield nickered as the wind shifted and a thick whiff of horse sweat slapped Sterling in the face.

"I know, I know. She's bossy and irritable, but she

would've insisted we rest after a full day's ride instead of boorishly pushing ahead like this. She has an annoying way of being right. You've kept impressive speed since the Great River, Banefield, and I'm sorry I pushed you too hard with little rest. Let's just walk for now. These roads are safe."

Sterling fumbled with a bag secured to his saddle and plucked a honey apple out of it.

"Well, walk and snack at the same time," Sterling clarified, leaning forward with the shiny, red fruit.

Banefield chomped on the treat, his favorite snack, and sauntered along the luminescent path, bobbing Sterling up and down over the smooth, round stones.

The Vionin Kingdom road curved around hills made of purple soil. Sterling enjoyed watching them rise taller in the distance, sporting pointy tops.

It's like watching mountains be born, he thought.

Winding their way over an arched bridge with ornate, metal fixtures, they were greeted by rainbow-fire torches and tiny goblin flies. Goblin flies were citizens of the Vionin Kingdom and one of several caretakers of the path—unlike their terrible, much larger cousins, the mountain goblins. Still, Sterling wasn't fond of them. Their elongated noses were crooked, and their beady eyes never blinked. It brought to mind the black glass jewels before that adorned a certain dark witch he'd faced. Sterling shifted uncomfortably in his saddle and pushed thoughts from his past back where they belonged.

Banefield halted within sight of the grand

entrance to the Vionin Kingdom. The royal gates were behemoth in size and gleamed in the dark, forged from Elvish pearls and blessed with ancient protection magic. They were a symbol of powerful light magic. But there was a problem. They were guarded by the most hideous living statues Sterling had ever set eyes on: two lizards as large as the gates themselves, carved from Grunne stone and gifted with some form of energy that brought them to life when someone approached. Sterling peered past the guards and caught sight of the princess's tower rising from the tallest point in the kingdom. It had been a few years since he'd had an audience with her, but he could still recall her floor-length hair and the way she tended to float when she was lost in thought. Focusing his hunter sight, he made out the space beneath her arched windows where dangling firefly plants hung, brimming with pops of orange light balls. But there was no sign of the princess. The wind shifted, and Sterling grimaced at the smell of his bearskin cape. Now wouldn't be a great time to run into the elegant heir to the Vionin Kingdom.

"Okay, this is close enough. We don't want to go to the gates this time, buddy," he whispered. "Cut around to the left."

Banefield hesitated, pulling his head toward the enormous lizard duo, likely craving a rest at the horse stalls and a smorgasbord of the finest horse feed within the safety of the kingdom walls.

"Banefield, no! C'mon, we need to go around.

Premadora said *not* to go in, didn't she? Time does strange things inside the kingdom—too many magical creatures and spells zooming around in there," Sterling said in a hushed voice. "Hey, I'll give you an extra honey apple as soon as we find a resting tree, hunter's promise."

Going at his slowest speed, Banefield waded through the tall field grass, and like a child throwing a tantrum, he thumped his heavy horse body haphazardly. A flurry of night moths burst from a bush as Banefield carelessly kicked it in passing.

"Could you be louder?!" Sterling hissed.

Banefield jolted up onto his hind legs. Too fatigued to activate his hunter's instincts, Sterling thumped against the hard ground like a sack of pecans.

"The witch hunter returns," a voice boomed.

Oh, no. The stone lizards are awake. Maybe if I lie here, they'll think I've left, Sterling hoped.

"Yes, indeed," said another. "But he does not seek passage into the kingdom on this journey."

"Is this true, Sterling Fierce? Or did you come all this way to hide in the field grass?" the first lizard thundered.

Reptilian eyes sparked with hints of blue flashes of lightning inside.

"Stand and show yourself. There are beetles that reside in that grass that would be delighted to burrow in your skin, a nice warm place to call home."

Skin beetles—worse than stone lizards, he quickly decided.

Sterling stood, wiping the dirt from his backside, and found himself limping as his legs adjusted to being out of the saddle after so many hours.

"Oh, hi, yes—just passing through to the Ice Lands, if you must know, and I know that you must," he replied, trying not to sound cross. "This does not concern the royal family, and I need nothing from the kingdom. I'm on strict Alins' business, and I'm in a hurry."

"Do you hear that complication in his voice? Something troubles the hunter," said one of the lizards. "We are wise. Ask us a question and you will receive an answer—but only one."

Banefield nuzzled Sterling toward the stone path. There was no use in hiding or fleeing. It was offensive to refuse the gift of a magical being, no matter how hideous they were to look at.

Sterling waded through the knee-high grass and used his hunter's sight to scan for any skin beetles.

"I mean no offense, but I would like to save my question for another time if that is acceptable to you both," Sterling said in his most polite voice.

The first stone lizard's eyes sparked a fiery blue flame. "He is overconfident. I could fix that," he growled.

"He isn't here to quarrel with us. He's on Alins' business—as he said. We shall let him pass and grant him one answer to a question of his choosing in the future," the second guard said. "And we must deliver the gift from Princess Aherin—it was a royal command."

Instantly, a tiny, round glass bottle appeared in his palm.

"It looks empty. What is this for?" Sterling asked, holding the bottle above the glowing stones.

"Invisibility potion, of course. Her majesty knew you were coming—and she's decided to help you. It would be proper to thank her at your earliest convenience," the second guard said.

Sterling nodded, storing the bottle in his pocket. He shook his messy brown hair out of his face, dislodging a few shredded blades of grass. Stormy gray eyes lit up, glowing beneath the dark brown curls as he looked into the giant stone lizard's eyes and nodded respectfully.

"I'll take my leave now. Thank you," Sterling said.

"He has changed. His blood has grown more powerful, but his mind wanders. Where it will go, not even he knows," the first guard spoke for the last time before shifting back into statue form once again. As quickly as the stone lizards had come to life, they fell silent, and their eyes darkened into hollow caves.

CHAPTER NINE
A HIDDEN DOOR

Sterling slept tucked into the nook of a giant Everen oak (far from any skin beetles) but was in the saddle again before daybreak. His mind raced, trying to forget the stone lizards and their offer to answer any question. Long after the kingdom towers blurred in the distance, Sterling found himself turning his head back. Once or twice, blue lightning flashed—probably just his imagination or lack of sleep playing tricks on him.

There could be no more delays on this quest. A girl's life was at stake, and witch or not, she could be saved if he mustered up the perfect plan. He needed to get in and out of the witches' hut as fast as possible. Like any hunt, there would be phases to the plan.

Phase one: get past the elder witches, fast, without detection, and my blood magic stays intact. Nobody gets blasted into dust, including me.

He would be able to find the elders—that would be

the easy part. But to sneak past the experienced witches, he'd need an incredible amount of luck, stealth, or an award-winning distraction. In his experience, dark witches recognized his presence easily, but he was unsure about light witches. This plan would depend on the elders' magic working against itself. Ensconced inside the enchantment that kept the Alin away, Evenna was hidden from the outside world, but Sterling's essence would also be hard to detect.

He fidgeted with the potion the princess had given him. It hadn't come with instructions, so he had no idea how long the invisibility would last. He would still need a distraction. He leaned forward over his horse's neck.

"Banefield, I have a favor to ask. If you help me, I'll make sure, back home, you get buckets full of honey apples—I'll even throw in a week's worth of fresh carrots from Uncle Roag's garden—a carton of turnips too." Sterling offered a tempting prize.

Banefield's ears twitched as he charged through the twisted pine forest, weaving around trees with grace. By the time the sun was high in the sky, Banefield's hooves were coated with wet, purple soil, and his breath was visible in the cold air. As they traversed the base of the mountains, snow blanketed much of the land, collecting puffy layers on the treetops. Sterling zeroed in on the snow crystals. From a distance, the frozen, white droplets appeared soft but magnified. The snowflakes were jagged configurations and never-ending patterns of diamonds, stars, and sharp angles that his hunter vision picked up effortlessly. It was joyful to see nature's creations, big or small.

Suddenly, Sterling's stomach hardened, and a chill swept through him. It was the familiar coldness of a nearby witch.

"Hey buddy, slow down. Let's find somewhere to rest. Head beneath the pines in case the snow gets heavier," Sterling instructed. He arched his back, but it didn't soothe the figurative boulder of ice in his gut.

"We're close. There are witches here. When we find their lair, I need to get inside, find Evenna, and get out without being seen, which means I need you to distract them. Remember that favor you agreed to do? Don't look at me that way—you agreed, remember? Your job is to keep the elders distracted for me. They must keep their eyes on you when I signal," Sterling explained. He dismounted and rummaged through his bags.

He pulled out a pointed shell. It had a cleverly crafted cover, which he unclasped so he could dump out its contents—dried fruit and a surprising amount of sand. Next, he plucked some pinecones and snapped a branch off a nearby pine tree. He waited a few minutes for sap to pool in the tree's new injury. He dipped the pinecones into the sap and shoved them together with the shell, creating a sticky pointy shape. He rolled this in Premadora's pouch, and when he removed it, it was covered in plendi dust and almost resembled a glittering unicorn horn. Sterling turned the pointy end up and slathered more tree sap onto the other end for good measure before heating it over a fire (quickly procured from his magic dagger) to dry the pitch into hunter's glue.

"This'll work."

Banefield shook his head and danced to the side. Sterling's hunter's instincts warned him of the horse's intention to "accidentally" step on his boots, and he bobbed out of the way. He popped back up, grinning as he held tight to the manmade unicorn horn.

"It'll only be worse if you fight it—and then it—won't be on—straight," Sterling said as he struggled to hold the horse's reins and glue the fake unicorn horn between Banefield's eyes.

Sterling's eyes teared up, and he held back a bout of childish laughter at the thought of Banefield dancing around like a unicorn, sap dripping down his head.

"You know, from the right angle, you really do look like a unicorn. Stay in the shadows, but make sure your horn can be seen from—here," Sterling framed an area of the open forest. "Once they see you, dodge their sight a bit, like a game of unicorn hide-and-seek. Pique their interest. Draw them out as far as they will follow you. I need time to get Evenna as far away as possible."

He dug through the saddlebags. "Here, you earned this," he said, opening a palm full of oats and burgle-berries he'd been saving. While Banefield munched sullenly, Sterling removed the saddle and stashed it with the saddlebags in the crook of a tree. Then he and his faithful horse began trudging through the frozen pine forest.

Coldness spread into Sterling's chest, tugging him toward a grove of trees with curled branches. One had an unusually thick trunk, and he instantly knew how to get to the witches.

"You're a good friend, Banefield. I just want you to know that."

Banefield kicked his back hoof in the dirt, swiped his tail, and huffed.

"Okay, I have to go. Wait for my sign and then start making some noise. The witches will be on high alert once I'm inside, but hopefully they'll be distracted enough. They should come outside and look for you. Give them a show—and a chase. Got it?" Sterling asked.

Banefield bobbed his head, and the unicorn horn wobbled slightly.

Every witch Sterling had met had lived in a hole in the ground like a burrowing rodent. Apparently light witches were no different. He instinctively slid his hand, scarred from past run-ins with witches, over the rippled tree bark of the largest tree in the grove. His eyes detected a glow from a ridge, and he followed it.

There should be a door—here.

His blood turned from cold to hot when his skin touched the tree knot handle. He eased the door open and slipped inside, ducking and taking a deep breath.

His blood began to pulse as the essence of witches' magic blended with the natural scent of loamy earth. A tree tunnel shifted into place, and he could stand without slouching. Sterling followed the tunnel as it curved into a dizzying figure-eight shape, all the while descending until the weight of the earth above him felt enormously heavy.

We're deep underground now. They should feel safe about this depth—there must be a living space nearby, he thought.

Blood pulsed rapidly in his forearms, and he paused, leaning against a giant tree root threaded with black-and-purple strands. "No, stay calm," he whispered, as his sharp hearing picked out shuffling noises. He closed his eyes and listened for the sound of breathing.

Three witches. One plump, short of breath; one old one with shallow breath; and one small one, farther away: Evenna.

The witch hunter's eyes swirled with streaks of stormy gray, and his blood felt like lava pulsing through his veins as he popped the cork of his tiny glass bottle.

CHAPTER TEN
INSIDE THE WITCHES' BURROW

Behind the curve of a massive tree root was a space that resembled an ordinary family room. It was incredibly dark despite Sterling's hunter's sight. His body looked watery and out of focus, even to his enhanced sight, proof that the invisibility potion was working. He tiptoed forward, keeping close to the solid trunk wall. The smooth, knobby wood was cold, but he didn't mind. The invisibility potion made his skin itch, and the cold was a relief. Plus, it balanced the coldness in his stomach.

He shifted his concentration, studying the open space. The room he was in was round, the live wood of the tree root grown around it. One wall opened into a wider space with a high ceiling that likely went up to ground level, where tiny pricks of sunlight peeked in. A staircase curled haphazardly from room to room, rising toward the surface with occasional doorways where hollow tree roots opened to create more rooms. The tree innards formed floors, ceilings, and walls with an irregular, wavy texture shaped by the natural bends of roots and littered with twisting mud vines.

In the family room, three chairs sat around a floating crystal block that cast a dim golden-brown glow. It was mesmerizing—but he assumed it was bewitched to something devious. On a nearby tabletop were glass beads of various sizes and ruby-colored powder sculpted into miniature pyramids. Untouched green-and-purple powder mounds sat on the opposite side, and a few beads had fallen onto the dust-coated floor. Stained cloth was strewn about the room, drooping from the chairs but mostly tossed into one big, messy heap.

Sterling's eyes widened, and his pulse thumped harder. An old witch was slouched in a chair with a pool of drool dripping from the corner of her mouth. She had to be the eldest witch. Her hat, too, looked centuries old—it even had wrinkles to match its owner. The sloppy hat sloped down her forehead, off-center, stained with green lipstick smudges that stuck out against mauve velvet. She reminded Sterling of Uncle Roag taking an afternoon nap. But still, Sterling's blood ran hot as if it would attack the old witch in her slumber at any moment. His spine tingled, and his eyes darted toward a rug made of animal fur, topped with the head of a bear. Its wild eyes trailed Sterling's every move. He tried not to flinch when it blinked.

Being inside this witches' hut is taxing my senses. I can't stay in here much longer, he thought. His forearms rippled as if lava bubbled beneath the surface. So far, his blood magic had obeyed him—but, like him, it was stubborn.

A clanging rang from the kitchen. Sterling crept forward to peek through the doorway. Bat wings and a string of tails hung from mud and stick cupboards. A short, heavyset witch clunked around cupboards and swatted at spider webs.

"Where is my eggshell cracker? It was here. Now, it's disappeared. Sheela, what have you done with my cracker?" demanded the plump but pleasant-looking witch, stuffing her thick, violet hair into a messy beehive-style bun and looking ready for business.

The hanging string of cattail reeds perked up and pointed toward the sleeping witch who smacked her lips.

"Did you lose something again, Tammilda?"

Cattails twitched back toward the plump witch as if they enjoyed the bickering and listened intently to the ongoings between their masters.

Tammilda wiped the sweat from her brow, then tightened her midnight-black apron around her bulging body.

Sterling took advantage of the ongoing quarrel and crept through the central chamber and into a spiraling hallway that led to two doors. The first was round and wide, like the plump witch. The second was askew, the frame off-center, warped, and heavily stained. This door must've belonged to the oldest witch. The plump one couldn't have squeezed inside if she was greased up with a cauldron full of frog oil. But there was no third door for a witch child. Sterling turned back toward the main chamber, but he couldn't sense any life in the rooms above. His blood burbled, signaling that the youngest witch was close, but where?

Evenna, you gotta give me a hint. Where are you? Sterling wondered, clutching his stomach, which may as well have been hosting an ice gremlin. He tried to remember the precise sound of her voice, the image of her face—anything to help him track her. He walked in circles, following the tree rings beneath him.

Suddenly, his head felt as if it would split open. He looked down as the hazy form of his hand began to solidify. The invisibility potion was wearing off. To make matters worse, his headache blurred his senses and he felt as dizzy as a spinning top. He slumped against the wall and closed his eyes.

"I bet all the stars in Everen's skies that eggshell cracker is in your room—stuffed away in a tree hollow!" Tammilda hobbled down the hall surprisingly fast for her size.

Wait, that's it! Sterling realized.

Hollows were small, but a young witch could fit.

Did I miss it?

He opened his eyes and held back a gasp. A set of handprints glowed like moonlight in midair.

Sterling's blood pounded behind his eyes, and Tammilda seemed to be breathing right behind him —impossible since he was still leaning against the wall.

The moonlight handprints pointed up.

Seconds later, the plump witch let out a squeal. Sterling froze, not daring to open his eyes.

"When was the last time you tidied your room? It's filthier than a goblin hole!" Tammilda bellowed. She stood facing Sheela's door, close enough that Sterling could have touched her twisting purple hair. Tammilda muttered a spell, and two eggshell crackers, a toad scraper, and a charcoal ladle flew to her, smacking into her sweaty palms.

"That's what I thought," she whispered, slamming the door shut and turning around. "And keep that door sealed. Your room stinks like human."

Tammilda began tucking the tools into her various pockets, never looking up to where Sterling was clinging to a series of trembling vines, prone against the ceiling. He wasn't invisible anymore, and he watched as a gigantic bead of sweat trickled down his nose. He shifted to the side, for the drop would land right on Tammilda. But then he was hoisted upward by his cape.

Sterling landed on a curved wood floor as a trapdoor clicked shut beside him. He rolled over, straining to see in the dark space, but before he could properly sit up, a glowing white band curled around his wrists, binding them together, then fastening his neck to the floor. The light wasn't painful, but it did tingle.

"I'm glad to see the snow leopard didn't tear you limb from limb, Sterling Fierce. But my elder witch keepers will not treat you as kindly if they find you here. You need to stop sweating. Tammilda will smell you, and she'll turn you into hunter stew," a familiar voice warned from the darkness. The sound barely echoed, and Sterling noted that the hollow was barely big enough for two people to lie flat next to each other.

"Stop sweating? How am I supposed to do that?!" Sterling began, but a cold, pale palm pressed against his mouth.

"Shhh!" Evenna scolded, but she removed her hand before commanding a gust of icy wind to blow over him, evaporating his sweat.

"There," she whispered, seeming pleased with herself. "I'm sorry about the restraints but I can't trust you yet."

Sterling sighed. In the blue light coming from his restraints, he glanced around the tree hollow. The air was thick with a scent like river grass and mud, which was nice. But it was cramped and had no natural light. At least the elders had a few light holes below.

While his stomach was still a ball of ice, he had no desire to destroy Evenna. For now, his blood magic agreed. "I won't hurt you. I'm here to save you—to take you to your grandfather, my Alin," Sterling whispered.

"Evenna! Breakfast!" Tammilda hollered from below, thumping against the trapdoor.

Sterling focused on what he could see of Evenna as she turned her wide-set, pale silvery-blue eyes on him. She bit her purple lips, and the pale, white-violet skin of her brow creased. Her delicate features seemed to glisten—her beauty radiated even in the shadows. She wore the same panicked expression he had seen in the Alin's magical portrait of her. She looked into Sterling's dark gray eyes for a moment.

"Open up or starve, girl!"

Evenna groaned as she released Sterling's restraints and shoved him aside as the trapdoor creaked open.

CHAPTER ELEVEN
A UNICORN SIGHTING

The trapdoor slammed shut as a bowl of eggshells and oat mush heaved upward, splattering into Evenna's hollow. The crude tree root bowl spun loudly until stopping in silence. Evenna didn't flinch or dodge the bowl, apparently used to having things thrown at her.

Now free, Sterling pulled out his horse whistle and blew. No sound came out, at least, no sound the witches could hear. Evenna looked at him quizzically, but he simply tucked the whistle away and focused his hearing on the sound of the elder witches below.

Outside, Banefield's ears twitched. He huffed a sigh, then pranced out of the trees and in plain view for the witches to see.

"Tammilda, you really must come see this!" Sheela squealed, scooching her creaky bones toward a wall where Sterling assumed they had a bewitched window.

Tammilda's heavy footsteps and panting faded down the bendy oak tunnel.

Sterling reached for the trapdoor, but Evenna hissed a warning. "Whatever you're doing, it's just going to make them angrier when they catch you. What did you do?" she demanded.

"There's no time to explain. You have to trust me. I can get you out of here, but we need to leave—right now," Sterling said as he pushed the trapdoor open a crack.

"We can't get past them!" Evenna hissed.

"Don't worry, phase three is the best part. I've created a diversion, but we're running out of time," Sterling said, offering his hand to her comfortingly. He'd seen fear in many creatures' eyes. She was terrified of someone or something—but not of him.

"Phase three?" she repeated in a shaky whisper, eyeing Sterling's outstretched hand, tanned, and riddled with scars.

Evenna gnawed at her lip as a tear trickled down her smooth, pale cheek.

"If they catch me, I'll be punished," she said shakily. She rubbed fresh welts on her wrist.

"You're already being punished. This *will* work," he said in his best calm voice. The elder witches were currently alternating between arguing and cooing. He grew more confident in his escape plan. The problem was convincing Evenna to trust him.

Sterling pushed the trapdoor all the way open, allowing Evenna to listen to her elders.

"I know that excitement in your voice! It's something wretchedly joyous! Maybe a family of lizards or snakes finally got caught in our trap. Yum!" Tammilda said.

"Did you feed the girl?" Sheela asked.

"Never mind about her. This is more important!" Tammilda moaned.

Evenna wiped a stray tear from her face and pulled her velvet cloak closer around her. The fabric caught the light the way crystal rock formations did in the moonlight. She took Sterling's hand, and they jumped down from the hollow.

Creeping along the curvy tree trunk walls, Evenna let Sterling pull her toward the family room. She halted just before the elder witches came into sight and tugged her hand away from his, but she didn't make a sound. Sterling peered around the corner. As he'd hoped, the witches were hovering by their enchanted window, shoving each other to get a better glimpse.

"It's most thrilling!" Sheela said.

Tammilda bobbed her head, which set most of her body jiggling warmly. "A unicorn! This is our prize for keeping balance in the magic realm—making sure the girl's power does not grow stronger. Locking her away was the best thing we've done in centuries."

"I doubted your decision, sister, but this is our sign. We removed the power imbalance and have been sent a reward—eternal life! Just one drop of unicorn blood is all we need," Sheela said, her eyes taking on a green glow.

Both witches cackled in unison as they vanished.

Sterling stepped into the deserted family room and glanced through the window. Despite his earlier resentment, Banefield looked like he was truly enjoying himself. He kicked up his heels and fluttered his long eyelashes. Then his ears pricked, and he trotted back toward the trees. He'd no sooner disappeared into the foliage when a pair of broomstick-wielding witches zoomed across the view. Sterling gulped. A blue glow sparked in the distance, Banefield's magic horseshoes.

"May speed be with you, my friend," Sterling whispered.

Sterling had done everything he could, and he trusted his horse. He glanced back toward Evenna to give her an encouraging grin. Her lips twitched like she wanted to smile, but her luminous eyes remained wide with fear.

Sterling absentmindedly scratched his palm. Instead of damp skin, his fingertips caught on something smooth and cold. He turned away from Evenna and glanced down. The space between his thumb and forefinger and a triangular section of his palm were crusted with overlapping black diamond-shaped scales.

Evenna's hand. I touched her hand.

"What's wrong?" Evenna whispered, sensing his discomfort.

"Nothing. We can go now. Let's get you far away from this place," Sterling said, turning his palm downward and out of sight.

Evenna nodded, lifting her cloak hood over her silky hair.

As the pair made their way through the winding tree tunnels and out of the witches' hut, the ice ball in his stomach began to melt. Once outside in the afternoon air, his mind refocused. Evenna scanned her rescuer, putting extra space between herself and him.

Sterling endured her scrutiny and tried not to feel self-conscious. He straightened his broadening shoulders and stood tall, noticing that he was just the right height so that if he were to hug Evenna, the top of her head would fit precisely under his chin. Her eyes caught on to the thin slash mark over his eyebrows, a parting gift from the snow leopard. It was healing quite nicely due to the sharpness of the attacker's claws. Sterling hoped it made him look tough, then realized he wanted to look reassuring.

"I made a promise to your grandfather, Evenna. I won't hurt you, and I won't let anyone else hurt you either," he promised.

Sterling and Evenna trudged through thicket and snow until they reached the rocky path west of the Vionin Kingdom. He thought it would be best to avoid the kingdom altogether. Having a witch, even a good one, out in the open was dangerous, and not just because the elders would be searching for her. Other magic doers may mistake her for a dark witch, and nonmagics might fear her.

Evenna squinted at the glaring light reflecting in the snow, but other than that, she seemed fine. Sterling caught her stretching her arms above her head, something she wouldn't have been able to do inside her tree hollow.

Once they were far enough out of range of the elder witches, both Sterling and Evenna relaxed a little. Sterling quickly found where he'd stashed Banefield's saddle. He'd hoped to find his horse in the same general area, but for now, he'd have to carry the saddlebags himself. He grunted under the awkward burden of the saddle, but he opted to keep moving. At least his hunter instincts were calm. He felt unexpectedly normal for walking with a witch.

So, how did you bewitch that bear all the way from that hollow? He was clear across Everen in the Artison Mountains, Sterling spoke in his mind.

It wasn't for sport, Sterling. It was terrible, and I'll never forgive myself, she said into his thoughts.

You did what you had to do to get your grandfather's attention—and it worked. But if you can freeze time, why not use that skill and escape? Sterling continued.

"You don't know much about witches," Evenna said aloud. "I figured you'd know all about us from hunter school."

"School? There's no school for hunters," Sterling

scoffed. "Anyway, I've only met dark witches, and I've destroyed all of them before we could exchange pleasant conversation."

Evenna huffed.

"Please don't ask me any more questions about my magic or speak of dark witches. They are still my sisters," she said.

"Yeah, well they aren't anything like you. But you're right, I don't know as much about witches as I should," he replied, glancing down at his blackened hand.

"What's that?" Evenna asked abruptly.

Sterling followed her gaze to a set of tracks in the snow.

"Fresh snow wolf prints, a pair of them. They are out hunting," he explained.

"I'm afraid of wild animals," she said.

As Evenna's face turned a shade paler, the black scales rippled around Sterling's fingers, completely covering them and stretching toward his wrist. He buried his hand in his pocket.

It's spreading, Sterling realized, searching for a pair of gloves.

Just then, the brush in front of them shook. Branches snapped, and a huge creature barreled toward them.

CHAPTER TWELVE
THE SHORTCUT

Evenna snapped her eyes shut, and Sterling dumped the saddle off his shoulders as he studied the shape emerging from the foliage. It was a lone animal, tall and powerful. He peered at it, but his hunter's instincts failed him until the beast was nearly on top of them. A stormy gray mane became clear as the shadow of a horse emerged.

"Banefield!" Sterling yelled, relieved to see his friend. But instead of being happy to see Sterling, the horse reared up and snorted in short bursts. A string of horse slobber slung straight toward Sterling's face. He ducked as the snot grazed the top of his head.

"Easy! What's wrong, buddy? I can't help if you don't calm down," Sterling insisted.

He looked over the horse. The only oddities were a few globs of tree sap and mud splashes on his silvery-white fur. The horn had broken off during Banefield's escape from the elder witches, and a jagged piece of pinecone remained stuck to his coat, gleaming like a real unicorn horn (if unicorns existed).

"I don't see any injuries," Sterling said, hugging the horse's neck. "Those witches just spooked you—gave you a real chase, huh? You really came through for me, again."

Banefield nudged Sterling and turned around, lifting his rear leg. Somehow, Sterling had missed it. There, as clear as Everen's stars, were bite marks, dripping with thick, crimson blood.

How did my hunter sight miss something so obvious?

Sterling was stunned. First, he hadn't detected the scent of his own horse like he normally would have. Then, right under his nose, he hadn't picked up the scent of blood or pungent tree sap on Banefield's fur.

"I'm sorry, Sterling. Witches do tend to attack if they do not get what they want," Evenna said, hanging her head.

"No—no, it wasn't your elders—the injuries are from snow wolves," the words stumbled from his mouth. He locked eyes with the young witch after examining the marks, trying to seem reassuring. But there was a more pressing matter to attend to. He cleaned the area around the gash as well as he could with melting snow, then ripped an empty food satchel into pieces long enough to wrap around the worst of the injuries.

"Alright, you'll be limping some, but the Alin will get you healed in no time, just as soon as we return to

Bren. This will have to do as a bandage for now," he said calmly as he tied a hunter knot.

Banfield neighed softly.

"You would've outrun a pack of snow wolves if you hadn't been helping distract the witches for me. It's my fault you got hurt, and I'm sorry. But because of you, Evenna was saved from that wretched tree hole. She's going to come home with us. She's a light witch—a good witch." Sterling rattled off facts, jittery from the uneasy feeling he had as the sun began to set.

"It's nice to meet you, Banefield. You are very brave for what you did," Evenna said, gazing at the horse, her eyes full of admiration. And Sterling blinked and turned away before she could catch him staring at her.

"Now that introductions have been made, we have a long journey ahead, and time isn't on our side. With an injured horse, the mountain trails aren't an option anymore. We'll have to cut south to the Vionin Kingdom roads. They are not well hidden like the mountain path, but they are easy to traverse. I was avoiding those roads because your elders may already be searching for you there. We'll have to hide you."

"We'll be sure to see a magic doer on the Vionin Kingdom roads. They're the most traveled in all of Everen. They'd find me there!" Evenna piped up.

Sterling rubbed his wrist where it had been smooth the last time he'd checked it. Now, beneath his sleeve, more scales grew, covering his wrist and part of his forearm. They spread every time Evenna seemed to be scared or distressed. He had to figure out a way to keep her calm or soon he'd be covered in thick, black reptile skin.

"I'll keep guard over you. Just lie down on Banefield like you're asleep—you are light enough for him to carry even with a hurt leg. And you won't slip out of the saddle if you hold on to the pommel. Trust me, I've had some great naps up there," he said with a wink, hoping that his casual demeanor would help convince her.

Evenna opened her mouth, looking like she wanted to protest, but Sterling anticipated her argument. "We'll ride for the kingdom roads now, but as soon as we find a better option, we'll take it. Hop on up and let's get you in position."

Evenna rode silently while Sterling hiked beside them, carrying the saddlebags to save Banefield from any extra weight. They arrived at the base of the mountains only a few miles from the kingdom roads just before sunset. Sterling repeatedly studied the black scales stretching up his wrist and thought it strange that they didn't hurt or itch at all despite their hideous appearance. In fact, he didn't feel his hunter's blood in that arm either—it was missing the usual thickness of his veins and the warmth of his magic. Then, it hit him like a dragon tail in the face.

Something is happening to my blood magic—it's being

siphoned by the scales, Sterling realized, eyeing Evenna as she rested.

Loose strands of waist-length, blue hair swayed, and her delicate nose tipped downward. It was hard to believe that she was capable of magic potent enough to damage his blood. She hadn't seemed to want to hurt him. Was this all an accident? How much worse would it be if she'd been trying to damage him? Feeling torn, he worried that Evenna carried darkness inside her, but he did trust what his Alin said—she was a good witch.

As the sun sank behind the mountaintops, Banefield nudged Sterling's scaly arm.

"What?" Sterling asked.

"I didn't say anything," Evenna replied with a delicate yawn.

"I meant the horse. He's just acting up—probably just hungry or something," Sterling explained, scooting forward out of reach of the horse's prodding nose.

"He probably doesn't want to go on the Vionin Kingdom roads either, do you boy?" Evenna said in a pouty voice.

Banefield sped forward, his enchanted horseshoes flashing with blue light. He nipped at Sterling's sleeve, nearly tearing the fabric near his wrist.

Stop. I'll be fine, Sterling said in his mind.

Banefield snorted in rebuttal.

"He is worried. He says his friend is sick," Evenna

said, sitting up in the saddle to get a better look at the witch hunter.

But Sterling marched ahead. "You speak horse too? Is there anything you can't do?" he snapped.

Evenna furrowed her turquoise eyebrows.

"I didn't mean it, Evenna. Well, I did mean it, but I'm sorry all the same. I don't like the idea of being out on the open road any more than you do. I just— we need to get to the Alin."

A flock of blackbirds flew overhead, squawking at one another.

"Even those birds could be spies sent to hunt us. Here, let's get you extra camouflaged. We'll be on the Vionin Kingdom roads in a half mile," Sterling said as he removed his tattered bearskin cape and put it over Evenna.

"This way, you look like a pile of goods being transported." He grinned, proud of yet another good idea.

"Thank you, Sterling. Thank you for listening to me in the Artison Mountains and thank you for saving me. You too, Banefield," Evenna said, nervously tracing a figure-eight pattern in the horse's fur.

Another batch of scales grew toward his shoulder.

"I know you're afraid, but I promise I will deliver you to your grandfather, Evenna."

Evenna sniffled beneath the bear cape, and Sterling hoped it was because of the bear smell and not because she was growing more nervous. After a few minutes, he turned back to see Evenna was weaving little braids into Banefield's mane. He decided not to comment. After all, she was trying to be kind, and they didn't look half bad. He ran his fingers through his own tangled locks. Maybe he'd let her braid his hair—but a traditional warrior-style braid, of course.

CHAPTER THIRTEEN
LOST ABILITIES

"We're only about five minutes away. I can feel the enchanted roads' magic. They are a sight to see, but my favorite part about them is the protection they provide—officially safeguarded by servants of the Vionin Kingdom, which means no trolls or goblins or fire dragons..." Sterling began.

"Or dark witches," Evenna cut in, her eyes briefly flashing glossy black, resembling a dark witch.

His veins pulsed intensely as a dreadful memory sparked in his mind, and he swallowed, trying to dislodge the icicle that seemed to have sprouted in his stomach.

No, he pleaded. But his blood magic flowed stronger, preparing to attack. *We don't want to harm the girl. She is not a threat.*

Magical waves pulsed through his body, and he gritted his teeth, but then it ebbed to a persistent but negligible hammering. His blood was warm, not hot. Evenna was not about to be diced into witch bits by a blood blade. His blood had heard him, and it listened.

But more blackened scales grew, stretching over his shoulder and prickling down his back.

His blood hadn't reversed flow or gone cold, which was a good sign. Yet his hunter instincts were disappearing from his body—and the scales had free rein to take over his skin, inch by inch. He shook his head. It was useless to try and explain it to Evenna. He didn't know as much about witches as he should have, but he recalled that witches were governed by their emotions. Knowing what she'd done, even unintentionally, would only create panic. She would become completely unstable.

Premadora hadn't mentioned anything about scales when she lectured him in her tiny, schoolteacher voice. For once, he wished she'd lectured longer.

Sterling stopped and turned to Evenna.

"Right, no dark witches would dare travel the king's roads. Since your elders are light witches, they can travel them anytime they like. But at least we won't have to worry about the worst sort of magical creatures—that's what I meant. Plus, the stones on the path glow. I like glowing stones," Sterling admitted with a boyish grin.

Evenna stared at him wide-eyed for a second, then seemed to relax into a tentative smile. Sterling wiped the silly smirk off his face and felt his ears turning red. He cast about for something to do and noticed a line of sap running down Banefield's neck. He swiped at it with his glove and tried to wipe the sticky mess off in a patch of grass. He scowled at a sudden realization. There was no odor—not of fresh grass, not of the usual overly sweet smell of the sap. There were loose clumps of white fur on the ground, but he couldn't smell them either, and his vision was too dull to tell him if the hair belonged to an elk, bear, wolf, or rabbit.

My hunter vision and smell...both are gone, he sulked in silence.

Banefield snorted and plodded on through the sparse foliage.

"So, what else do you know about the kingdom roads?" Sterling asked Evenna, trying to distract her as he caught up and pressed his face into Banefield's sweaty neck and took a deep inhale.

For the first time in his life, he smelled nothing.

"I've seen them in my visions," Evenna replied without emotion. "I, um, wasn't allowed to travel, so I imagined myself going. That's how I saw you in the Artison Mountains too. And how I bewitched that poor bear. My grandfather had messaged me before the elders blocked all magical communications. He mentioned you, and I thought maybe you could tell him about me. I hadn't anticipated the snow leopard. Oh, that poor bear! It just makes me sick—so many innocent creatures died because of me. But I was scared that if I didn't get out, something worse would happen."

Sterling half listened, consumed with finding out if he'd lost his sense of smell completely.

"Well, you got out before something worse came of your situation. You did what you had to do to survive—as a hunter, I understand that more than you know. And you'll see the enchanted roads soon. We're almost there—should be able to see them once we get out of this last thicket," Sterling confirmed.

He shoved his face into Banefield's silky fur for a second time. This time, the horse cricked his head and snorted. In horse speak, this meant "knock it off."

"Yeah, sorry, just lost my balance. So, Evenna, you can travel anywhere you want in your visions?" Sterling asked, trying desperately to keep her from noticing his panic.

No more scales, no more scales...

He scanned the brush to search for anything he could try to smell. The sun was casting its final rays through the bare winter tree branches, but Sterling's night vision wasn't activating. He let out a shaky sigh, but then his gaze landed on a set of fresh paw prints.

"Evenna, hang on to the reins. Fresh wolf prints— hang on tight." Sterling tried to keep his voice calm, but Evenna gasped as something thrashed behind a pair of thorny shrubs. Two snow wolves emerged, snarling as they focused on the horse's meaty hind legs. Banefield reared up, and Evenna flung her arms around the horse's neck, desperate to hold on.

Sterling jumped between his friends and the pair of hungry wolves, locking eyes with the wild animals. Both were female. One had a brown eye and a blue eye—the other a pair of piercing yellow eyes and a badly disfigured mouth. He didn't need hunter's sight to see their ribs sticking out and bald spots where clumps of snow-white fur had fallen out.

"Do something!" Evenna shouted, barely hanging on to Banefield as he bucked and kicked.

Banefield's neigh rang out, echoing against mountain rock and pine trees.

"It's not their fault. They're sick from starvation," Sterling replied calmly as he rummaged through one of the saddle pouches slung around his neck as more scales spread across his shoulder.

"Look, I know you're hungry, but you can't eat the horse. He's my friend," Sterling said to the wolves in an attempt to reason with them and lull them into a calm state—an old hunter trick that may only last a few seconds, but he hoped that was all he needed.

The wolf with bicolored eyes howled to call the rest of her pack. A ridge of snow-white fur rose along her spine. Then, she pounced clear over Sterling's head with visions of horse steak dancing in her eyes.

Sterling used his speed reflexes (at least he still had those left) to leap into the air. He nudged the wolf, knocking her off course, and tossed a chunk of dried bear meat smack into her nose. The dazed wolf shook her head. Clumps of what must have once been sleek fur drifted to the ground as she pounced on the bear jerky.

Sterling's legs began to shake, and he felt the tingling of black scales writhing down his thighs. The scales were absorbing his abilities at a faster rate, and his body grew weak.

"Let's go before the pack gets here. We're fresh out of bear meat," he said, pulling himself onto the saddle behind Evenna.

"What are you doing? You're too heavy for Banefield to carry!" Evenna shrieked.

"Can't...explain. Banefield, RIDE NOW," Sterling's voice slurred. He reached around Evenna to take the reins but slumped forward instead. His vision blacked out, and he wasn't sure he was even conscious anymore.

He had lost his instincts—the abilities he'd inherited from his father and the skills he'd been honing for the past few years. It was all slipping away. And more than that, his body was changing into something unfamiliar, and every ounce of him felt depleted. For the first time, he wasn't sure if he'd make it home again.

Banefield galloped with a significant limp, likely in a great deal of pain, along the last stretch of the trail before bursting into the light of the Vionin Kingdom road. The evening sun cast an orange glow over the land, and the howling of wolves pricked at his nerves.

CHAPTER FOURTEEN
THE SILK-WEARING MERCHANT

S terling awoke to the sound of thunder. A gray blanket of clouds spun overhead as nightfall set in. Sterling sat up from his nap in the saddle and stretched to loosen the muscles in his back. He realized that Evenna wasn't next to him. Instead, she walked alongside Banefield wearing her hooded silver cloak. He blinked at the embroidered mint-green flowers, which he hadn't noticed before. Quickly, he lifted his pant leg out of sight and caught a glimpse of what looked like mini-dragon scales wrapped around his calf. He covered the hideous markings and looked out onto the enchanted roads, rainbow-fire torches burning in the distance.

Banefield had outrun the snow wolves despite his injury, and they were well on their way to the Alin. Squinting down the Vionin Kingdom path, Sterling saw moving figures, travelers of sorts.

"You look out of place—saddle up and stay hidden

beneath my cape. You need to appear like a pile of goods. That was the plan," Sterling said.

Evenna giggled. "Well, you passed out. The plan changed, but I've managed just fine while you were in dreamland over there. You know, you talk in your sleep."

"I do not," Sterling said under his breath.

He jumped down, thankful that the scales didn't inhibit his movements. He couldn't help but smile as the stones beneath his boots reacted with each step, glowing brighter.

I really do love these roads, he thought.

"What are you doing?" Evenna asked. Banefield seemed to roll his eyes, but he kept going as Evenna planted herself in the path in front of Sterling.

"Nothing—just testing out my strength. Weren't you supposed to be doing something to keep yourself safe until I can get you to your grandfather?" he quipped, giving her a concerned face like the one his father had given him on night hunts when he'd ventured too far astray.

Evenna scanned his face, worry creating a crease on her otherwise elegant brow. Then she sighed and caught up to Banefield.

"I don't mind lying up here, but your cape stinks like bear urine," she whined, holding her nose shut.

"Welcome to the great outdoors," Sterling said with a smirk.

They traveled the rest of the night southwest along the Vionin Kingdom roads, keeping ahead of the rain. Evenna sulked in silence in fake cargo position while Sterling marveled at the multicolored flame torches and the occasional patrol fairy or goblin that would leave sparkles in its wake.

It didn't take long for a passerby to comment on Banefield's limp once the sun rose the next morning.

"The snow wolves are starved, and they will come after horses or mules—anything with meat. Stay safe if you venture into the mountains," Sterling would warn.

He was met with half smiles and uncertain looks by most other travelers. They probably questioned why someone rich enough to own a horse like Banefield would be hauling goods in the middle of the night. But most of the travelers on these roads were merchants in standard travel boots, reused tattered capes, and hats faded from being worn too long in sunlight. They were in a hurry to transport their wares from one place to the next, so they politely moved on without probing further.

"There's one big curve ahead before the Vionin Kingdom path ends. We'll take that, then cut between the Dark Forest and the Swamplands. Banefield will need to get some lift to activate his water-walking enchantment. Once his horseshoes are charged, he'll be able to carry us over the marsh all the way to the Great River," Sterling explained.

But Evenna did not respond.

"Hello?" he asked, lifting the cape.

Evenna's eyes were closed as she slumbered. Her face looked peaceful, and it shimmered a periwinkle hue he'd only seen in the race of elves.

That can't be. My senses must be going haywire, Sterling thought. Banefield snorted, and Sterling realized he'd been staring for nearly a full minute. He blinked and dropped the cape hastily. It settled gently over Evenna's petite frame once more.

As they rounded the familiar curve, the last leg of the enchanted roadway, one last merchant came into view. The man was not elderly but also not a young man by any means, and he seemed unhurried, a contrast to the others before him. He wore a navy-blue suit made of silk (even the buttons had silk sewn over them) and a slanted cap that tilted precariously on his head, somehow, without tipping over. The cap was made from the same silk, and his cloak too. This merchant was pudgy around the middle and his short stature didn't do him any favors.

But his mustache was a rosy hue and curled midway up his round face, giving him a friendly appearance almost instantly. He rode in a cart with brass edges and solid wood wheels, pulled by seven donkeys. The donkeys must have been related because they each bore the same marking on their chest, a triangle of white fur.

"Good day to you, son," the silk-wearing merchant spoke with a melody in his words, and the scent of rose petals and tropical fruit filled the air.

"Good day, sir," Sterling replied, resisting the urge to check if Evenna was hidden. He had been hoping the silk man spoke a foreign language so there would be no occasion for conversation.

The donkeys slowed to a stop, the sign of inevitable chat or impromptu sales pitch.

"Are you in the market for something special?" the merchant asked with a pleasant smile.

"No thanks, but I appreciate you taking the time," Sterling said, making eye contact to show he had nothing to hide.

"Oh, I don't mind sparing time for a traveler such as yourself—a nice young man out in Everen, earning a living," said the man as his mustache perked up even higher. "You may think I sell regular leather goods or hearth wood—something like that. Am I right?"

"To be honest, yes. But I really must be on my way," Sterling said politely.

"I'm not a regular in these parts. I've traveled a good way, but imagine! Destiny has brought our paths across each other's at this very moment. You may be interested to know that I sell only the finest wands in Everen. For yourself or a wizard friend, perhaps?"

Sterling thought of his friend, the potion wizard, and he suddenly felt compelled to buy a wand for him. Truly, this meeting could have been the result of fate, he realized.

"Well, I do have a friend who collects obscurities. Do you have one made of ancient wood or anything a bit on the rare side?" Sterling inquired.

"Pssssst," came a hiss beneath Sterling's bear cape. Banefield stomped his hoof against the stone path.

But Sterling ignored his friends, struck with anticipation as the wand salesman reached into the back of his cart.

He emerged, rosy mustache perked up and curled at the ends, holding a container filled with slender, rectangular boxes. Each box had carvings etched on the top with different symbols.

"That one!" Sterling exclaimed.

He pointed at a plum-colored box with a symbol of a dragon etched deeply into the wooden cover. "That's the one I want for my friend. He's a great wizard—the most talented potion wizard in Everen."

"You have an eye for the peculiar. This wand is a rare one indeed. Do you see the etching? It's carved from the scale of a bewitched dragon. Even a foul creature such as a dragon can fall victim to the evil of witches. One can never be too careful around a witch. Do you agree?" The merchant's face shifted, and his mustache fell limp, forming a beard with curled, twisted ends instead.

"I—I agree, sir," Sterling repeated in a robotic voice, feeling as though he was no longer in control of his words.

Snap out of it, Sterling! He's a wizard—a shape-shifter. You're in terrible danger. We must leave his presence at once! Evenna shouted in her mind.

Banefield chomped hard on Sterling's elbow.

"Ow!" Sterling finally responded, rubbing his arm.

He felt as if he'd just awoken from a dream. When Sterling looked back at the merchant, he saw his true form—a hooded man with a bushy black beard hanging past his lumpy stomach. The man's fingertips were half human-looking and half talon. His mouth pointed outward from the rest of his face, sloping into a curved beak. His human nose flattened beneath solid white eyes with no pupils. And he did not smell like roses and fruit anymore.

"Hand over the witch, and the dragon wand is yours!" the bird-like wizard squealed.

A wave of desire washed over Sterling, and he took an involuntary step toward the wand.

Breaking eye contact with the hooded figure, Sterling shouted, "No! There will be no trade, and there is no witch here."

A cackle echoed from the beak as the wizard shoved the plum box toward Sterling's gloved hand. Flames burst up from the contact. As holes burned through the glove, his scaled skin was revealed.

"There's no denying the girl's power—she is wicked! Look at what she's done to you already! Give her to me and save yourself while you still can!" the wizard screeched.

Sterling smacked Banefield's hind leg, sending him into a gallop, taking Evenna as far away as possible as he stood his ground. How had this devious creature gotten past the kingdom's protections?

"You can't keep her from me!" the wizard huffed, fumbling through his array of wands. He pointed a curled, white-barked wand at Evenna, and sparks began fizzling around the tip.

"It's not you I'm keeping her from—it's ME!" Sterling shouted as his blood magic burst from his one unscaled forearm. Bright red rope circled around all seven donkeys, binding them into a panicking, hee-hawing pack of confusion. Then, a blood spear was whizzing toward the enemy's heart.

"Be gone, wizard—if you deserve to be called one," Sterling hissed.

"You will regret this witch hunter—if *you* deserve to be called one" the wizard cried out as he and his seven identical donkeys vanished instantaneously into a flash of purple lightning.

CHAPTER FIFTEEN

ADMITTING THE TRUTH

Sterling found himself lying on his back in the middle of the Vionin Kingdom road. His mind whirled with the image of the wizard's soulless eyes and deformed, beaked face. He knew there were dark wizards in Everen, having fought one before, but it was always jarring to see evil magic up close.

It didn't help that his sight was blurred after the wizard's vanishing powder had exploded in his face. It felt like someone had dumped fistfuls of sand inside his eyes.

The shape-shifter wizard used vanishing powder to escape—but to where? And how did he break the road's protection seal? Sterling wiped his face with his shirt sleeve as residue smeared it with dark purple streaks.

But all that really mattered was that the wizard was gone and Evenna was safe—wasn't she?

"Evenna!" he shouted as he lifted himself to a

seated position and swiveled his head to search for her.

He blinked hard to encourage the scratchy debris out of his eyes, and the world around him sharpened a little. Thunder boomed and jagged lightning bolts ripped through dark clouds. The storm had caught up, and the sky let loose. Instead of rain and wind pummeling his face, translucent pearls floated down like soap bubbles dancing over a sudsy laundry bucket. They landed on his nose in a neat pile like an upside-down stack of clear bunches of grapes.

"Take it easy, hunter," a soft voice commanded. "You were right about the enchanted roads. They can protect us—even from the rain."

Evenna's delicate facial features came into view as she crouched to look him over. Her eyes had a tinge of panic inside, but that wasn't unusual for the young light witch. As she leaned across him to brush a clump of bubbles off his ear, a lock of bright teal hair escaped from her cloak.

An exceptionally rare hair color. I've only seen it once in my travels, he thought. *Inside the Elvish castle—a pure color, only found in the Elvish race.*

"Your hair," he managed to get out before Evenna tucked it beneath her embroidered hood. Falling bubbles perched on her silver cloak before sliding down its rounded edges without so much as dampening the cloth.

"And that's some magical cloak—"

"Sterling, can you remember anything after the explosion?" Evenna interrupted.

"My blood magic attacked him—I didn't want to use it anywhere near you," Sterling began, forgetting about Elvish hair or enchanted cloaks.

"Wait—why is my pant leg tugged up?" he hollered before snatching the material and pulling it over his scales.

His deep gray eyes swirled with mini storm clouds inside. "You have no right to pry into my personal, uh, person. That doesn't make sense, but you know what I mean!"

"I'm sorry, but this looks serious. Banefield and I— we were worried. There are black scales spreading across your body. Did the wizard do this to you?" Evenna asked, biting her lip.

"No," Sterling replied, letting his head plunk into his palms. "They were there before—do you know what they are?"

Evenna's eyes glossed with tears as she squeaked out the words, "It's been a long time, but I know snake scales when I see them. Why didn't you tell me?"

"I wanted to get you to the Alin where you'd be safe. I can worry about this later," he said somberly.

"No, you can't. You need a healer now!" Evenna exclaimed, sounding as bossy as Premadora.

Banefield nudged Sterling, helping him to his feet.

"Thanks, buddy. Look, Evenna, I can tough it out for now. I'll be fine until we get to Bren. The Alin's a great healer. He'll know what to do," he said, straightening his pant leg and frowning at the burnt glove. Dark snake scales gleamed through the holes, but there wasn't much he could do.

I hate snakes, he thought.

"You may not have time. How long have you had them? Did you touch something that has a personal connection to my elders? Snake scales are a common protection curse that many witches use."

"I'll tell you, but you won't like it," Sterling said with a sigh, signaling for Evenna to hop into the saddle so they could continue their journey. He realized that she hadn't heard the dark wizard's warning, and part of him was relieved. At least he could tell her gently.

Evenna bit her cheek and nodded, obeying his request and even covering herself with the bear cape without being reminded.

"The scales appeared after you took my hand in the elders' hut. They spread every time you get upset or scared—when your emotions are strong. I'm sorry, Evenna. I didn't want to make things more complicated," Sterling said, walking alongside Banefield, thankful he didn't have to see the mix of emotions on Evenna's face.

"It's not your fault," Evenna replied, shaking the cape from her head so that she could meet Sterling's eyes. "It's my fault that I can't control my magic." Her complexion pulsed with a purple glow.

Sterling's blood stirred.

"Please don't activate any magic around me—try

not to think of any big emotions like anger or sadness. Your magic tempts my blood," he begged. "It's hard enough to hold back my instincts as it is."

"I didn't—" she started but froze as Sterling gasped for air.

Scales were climbing down his other arm now and up the side of his neck.

Evenna pulled the cape over her head and burst into sobs of apologies.

Emotional things, witches. I don't know why I thought she would be different, Sterling thought.

He concentrated, calming his blood once again and refocusing on returning to Bren as quickly as possible. Sterling heard his father's words: "A hunter must always honor his word and complete his quest. If he fails, he cannot return home. It's hunter code."

Thunder popped as the sky blackened. Banefield neighed, signaling that more travelers were ahead. Sterling peered at the cart. There were two men in hooded capes seated on a small wagon pulled by a trio of mules.

"Something is not right," Sterling said, picking at the scales on his neck. He froze. "Evenna, you asked me what I remembered before the wizard disappeared. This is it! The triangle markings on his donkeys are just like the markings these travelers have. We're being hunted. We have to leave this road!

"Banefield, cut south and take Evenna to the Great River. I'll meet you there. I'm going to stay here—I will distract them."

Wild, pale blue eyes met his. "No, we ride south to the castle of the elves. They have ancient healing magic. I made you sick, and I am responsible for your healing," Evenna insisted.

"If we go that far off course, I can't guarantee your safety," he admitted.

"My safety isn't guaranteed anywhere. Let's go— the elves will heal you and mend Banefield's leg," Evenna demanded.

The two hooded men were drawing near, their eyes glowing deep purple (a wizard's color). They sensed Sterling's hesitation and raced their mules forward, their cart sparking at the wheels.

Sterling mounted his horse behind Evenna and tugged on the reins.

"Then we ride south to pay a visit to the elves," he said, placing his free hand on his dagger.

CHAPTER SIXTEEN
THE FORK IN THE ROAD

Hooves pounded across fields of knee-high grass, the horse avoiding large stones that loomed up in the dark—a difficult ride compared to the smooth kingdom roads. The wilds of Everen were beautiful but unpredictable. Banefield had to tread carefully, but time was running out. They were all weary, and Banefield's limp was more pronounced, but their best option was to get to the elves as fast as possible.

Lukewarm rain pummeled against them, and a warm breeze blew Sterling's hood down. The fresh rainfall rinsed sweat from his brown locks, and he happily drank raindrops as they rode. The snake scales had siphoned most of his hunter instincts, and it pained Sterling not to smell the fresh rain. But being in nature was still refreshing, and it was nice to leave the cold of the mountains behind.

Not long after the Vionin Kingdom castle fell out

of sight, they finally returned to something resembling a road. Banefield trudged through the mud and finally clambered onto the packed earth. The road was shrouded in early morning darkness, but not far off, it forked. Sterling peered between their options, but something behind them caught his eye—a pair of glowing lights. But he couldn't be sure, not with such diminished instincts. It could be glowflies or some other creature, curious or lost.

Whatever it is, they shouldn't be out in the rain, he thought to himself, careful not to mention his suspicions to Evenna.

Evenna had begun to regain control of her emotions, but Sterling didn't know how much longer he could restrain his blood. The snake scales were taking over his body, leaving him weak, on the outside, at least. On the inside, it felt like he was carrying a wild animal. He feared he couldn't control his blood for much longer, and it might attack Evenna. If they could reach the elves quickly, they could help. But getting to the Elvish castle wouldn't be simple.

"Which way are we going?" Sterling yelled through a splatter of raindrops. Thunder drowned out Evenna's reply. When the rumble faded, Evenna shouted back.

"What do you mean?" She looked around warily.

"Remind me to give you a map of Everen—you'll need it now that you're free to roam. Listen, we have two options to get to the elves. We can travel through the Cannabie Desert where the rain won't follow. But we may run into a sand dragon there," he began.

"What's the other option?" Evenna asked hastily.

Another crack of thunder rang out.

"We face the Swamplands and hope to Everen's stars that the venomous fly season has passed," he said. "It's all the same to me if you want to pick."

While Evenna squirmed and considered her options (all while trying to keep her emotions calm), Sterling peered at his rain-drenched sleeves. They clung to his arms, exposing the scaly texture beneath. Normally, two blue-ink tattoos would have been visible on his wrists. One—a faded crescent moon nestled into a cloud, was a symbol of the mother he'd never met. The other—a hunter's bow, a symbol of his father. The scales had covered them both, stealing his human skin and part of his identity like a black eraser.

Evenna shouted in his ear. "I choose the safer path —the one without dragons."

But he hadn't heard her. He was lost in thought as a pang of emptiness fluttered in his chest.

These scales have transformed me into a walking reptile, he thought.

"Hey, what are those symbols?!" Evenna exclaimed.

Sterling's eyes widened as he snapped back into the present.

"You can see them? Are you using witch's sight or something?" Sterling accused.

"Of course I can see them. They are beautiful—

pure white light piercing through your shirt. I'm not using any magic," Evenna said as her voice trailed off.

He pushed his sleeves up and to his surprise, Evenna was right. He hadn't seen the Elvish markings since the day the Elvish queen herself had placed them there. In all this time, they had never shown themselves. But now, two Acreedian dragon symbols glowed like starlight.

"I, um, yes. The elves," he stammered as he examined the symbols and neglected to apologize for his irritable tone a moment ago.

"Why do you have Elvish markings on your skin? And why are they glowing?"

Fair question. But there wasn't time to explain.

"I haven't always chosen the safest path, but dangerous roads can lead you to unexpected places," he replied, unrolling a pocket-sized map.

"This is where we are." He pointed to what looked like a jam stain on the map. Sterling was never sure if his uncle's maps were magicked to show his location or if there were just so many stains that one was bound to appear wherever Sterling was standing. "East takes us to the sands. South leads into the swamps," he said.

Evenna nodded toward the south.

"The lady has spoken—and she chooses the safer, dragon-free path," he teased, secretly wishing she'd chosen the sands. At least he was familiar with traversing them, and he wasn't scared of dragons.

With a tug of the reins, they sped over a combination of land and water that slowly molded into the same hue of mustard green. Beneath them, the path disappeared under stretches of murky water, only to appear again whenever there was high ground. From afar, the swamp's smooth-barked trees appeared calm. Their trunks sprouted lumpy branches at all heights the way a child would draw a picture using a mess of random squiggles.

Soon they were barreling through the dark under a lush canopy of trees, a refuge from the rain. Any residual solid ground melted away. Banefield's enchanted horseshoes glowed pale blue as he hovered above the swamp water. It was like riding across a bowl of pea stew, except it smelled worse. In the dark, it was difficult to tell what was water, mud, or boggy ground except where plants sprang up, and even then, it was unclear where the water ended and the foliage began. Although it was raining as hard as ever, the sound was muffled by layers of pale green leaves.

"This place gives me an eerie feeling, and the color of the water is disorienting. I can't tell the ground from the sky, and the trees are all crossing into each other—the vines look like tree serpents," Evenna whispered.

Sterling eyed his serpent-like skin and silently brushed off the unintentional insult. He also didn't want to admit he'd never actually been inside the swamp. Without his hunter instincts, he kept a diligent focus on anything that moved or that might want to sting, bite, or drag them beneath the mossy olive-green waters.

"Sterling. Psst!" Evenna whispered.

"What?"

"Do you hear that noise?"

"No, but I'm not used to using my human senses—wait, I hear something now," he said, turning his head toward a low buzzing sound coming from behind them.

Something big flew straight toward them. Whatever it was, it was coming fast.

CHAPTER SEVENTEEN
SWAMP SLUDGE

"Is it a swarm of venomous flies?!" Evenna cried.

"I don't know," Sterling began as Banefield jerked his head to one side then the other.

"Banefield, stop going in circles," Sterling commanded as he strained to identify the incoming creature.

The horse kicked his hind legs back and then swung his head wildly. His movement sent swamp water splashing and clumps of algae flung into the air. Sterling struggled to keep himself and Evenna in the saddle while the buzzing throbbed in his ears and his innards vibrated.

I can't see, Evenna said in his head, echoing in Sterling's thoughts.

A purple light flashed with the intensity of a midday sun. He closed his eyes, blinded by the brightness, and his hand slipped from the reins. Plucking his dagger from his waist, he pointed the blade toward the coming intruder. Instead of gleaming a blue glow, the edge of the blade sparked with red flame, a gift from his dragon brother—something the snakeskin couldn't take from him.

A deafening explosion popped overhead. Sterling felt Evenna slip from his grasp as they tumbled into the swamp water. He twisted and spluttered, quickly regaining his footing. Buzzing vibrated in the air, and he sank low. He tried to focus on the splashing sounds, but everything had gone dark, and he had no idea where Evenna and Banefield were in the chaos.

Then everything went still, and all Sterling could hear were light raindrops plunking off leaves or dropping into the scummy water.

"Sterling? Is it gone?" Evenna's soft voice rang out, echoing off the rippling water. He followed her voice and made out the shimmering outline of her silvery cape. She seemed to be clinging to a wide exposed tree trunk rising out of the swamp water a few horse lengths away.

"Yes," he replied. "I didn't know your cloak could fly—glad you're okay. Can you see Banefield?" He scanned the yellow-green water for his horse.

Sterling's chest sank when he saw the top half of Banefield sticking out of a pool of mustard-colored sand. His enchanted horseshoes were buried beneath its depths, trapped.

"Swamp sludge—Banefield will drown if we don't help him," Sterling hollered. He didn't care if he disturbed every wood sprite and venomous fly in the whole swamp right now. He careened through the swampy water until he was as close as he dared get. He knelt and reached for Banefield's bridle, but the reins were just out of reach. The ground gave way beneath his knees, and he stumbled back.

Evenna's eyes bulged in panic as her cloak wrapped around her body.

"What do we do?"

"Can your magic cloak pull him out?" Sterling pleaded.

"I'm sorry, but it's bound to me. It can't protect anyone else. I wish that it could," she said, biting her cheek.

"Fine. Just keep an eye on him and yell if the sludge gets to the base of his neck," he interrupted and stumbled through murky water toward a grove of trees enveloped in vines. He whacked and sliced away green spider webs until the vines were exposed. He tugged with all his strength, but algae drippings caused the vines to slip out of his grasp.

"I need a rope to pull him out. Evenna! Use your magic—here," he said sternly.

"But..."

"Do it and do it quick!" Sterling said in a strained voice, jerking on the vine.

Snap!

Sterling tumbled into the water again, his eyes dazzled by the white light that had popped overhead just before the vine broke. His blood began to boil in response to witch magic.

No, he commanded. But his blood emerged from his forearm and formed a dozen glossy red arrows. They turned toward Evenna and twitched in the air.

Stop—leave her alone. He willed the blood arrows to strike the muddy swamp's edge, and they reluctantly turned and darted into the swamp sludge, releasing Banefield's front legs. He struggled, but his back legs were still stuck in the deadly slush. Sterling willed the arrows to dig beneath the swamp once again, hoping he could find some leverage to save his frantic steed. He tied a sturdy knot in the vine and tossed it around Banefield's neck.

"I got you, buddy," Sterling said, taking care to avoid tightening the rope against Banefield's windpipe. He heaved with all his might, and Banefield thrashed, finding a few stout roots that gave him a slight ledge of footing.

"Hurry, Sterling! That light is coming back!" Evenna cried out as the buzzing noise returned. Sterling promptly recognized the faint purple glow. He redoubled his efforts, leaning so far back, he nearly tipped backward into the water.

"Not yet! I've almost got him...I won't leave him," Sterling said as he wrapped the vine around his waist and leaned backward, slower this time. Then Banefield wrestled one front leg out of the muck. Sterling nearly cried with relief. With one hoof firmly planted on a flat stone, Banefield leaned against the rope and stood, putting all his weight on the front leg. Sterling nearly toppled into the swamp again as his horse broke free of the sandy goo. He shook his mane and tail, sending clumps of sludge splattering through the air. From beneath his hooves, the blood arrows flattened and returned to Sterling's arms, their mission completed. But the last one paused, pointing straight at Evenna.

That's enough, Sterling commanded.

The arrow reluctantly returned to its home just as purple light drenched them in one giant purple-red shadow. Whatever it was, it had zeroed in on the three of them.

"Sterling! We need to go," Evenna whispered, peering into the sky toward the glowing ball of light.

Sterling nodded and reached for the slippery leather reins. But before he could get a sturdy grip, Banefield's nose flared. The vine had grown taught against his neck.

"Something's wrong," Sterling said.

The sludge tugged on the vine, angry that it had lost its dinner, and pulled it downward as a hideous slurping sound bellowed from the pit. Sterling's blood magic rose, cutting the ropey vine from Banefield's throat, but the severed end whipped in circles before pelting Sterling in the stomach on its return. Knocked off balance and without hunter instincts to save him, Sterling tipped over and fell headfirst into the sludge hole.

A hot wetness smacked against his face, and he tensed his shoulders to try to paddle to the surface, but it was useless. The wet, itchy sand held him in place.

Think, Fierce. There must be a way out. Fight your way out, he thought.

The more he wiggled his legs in the air, the deeper his head, shoulders, and stomach sunk into the pit. He was running out of air, and the carnivorous sludge squeezed his chest as it likely had done many times to other unfortunate creatures that fell into its lurches. There was no fighting his way out.

Sterling, please don't hate me for this, Evenna's voice said in his mind, but it was faint and garbled. Then, he blacked out.

The next thing he knew, he was facedown in the swamp water, his face tangled in someone's hair. He reared back and gasped a huge lungful of air. His leg burned, the witch-hunter blood boiling.

"Evenna!" he choked out, realizing that he must have collapsed on top of her. The last patch of human skin tingled on his face as the scales spread, covering it completely and cooling the burning of his blood. But he didn't have time to worry about that as he pulled her limp body out of the shallow water. She'd used her magic to save him, and somehow the purple light had gone—probably retreated after catching sight of Evenna's magic.

Sterling surveyed the petite body in his arms. Her skin had turned stark white. Her eyes were closed, and to anyone else, she would've appeared to be asleep.

"She's hurt—maybe she drained her energy getting me out," Sterling said desperately. His hunter instincts, whatever were left, told him the limpness in Evenna's body meant that something far worse had happened.

That's when he spotted it. A blood dart had pierced her neck.

"No!" Sterling screamed. "That wasn't supposed to happen!"

The dart wriggled out of Evenna's skin at his command and flew back to him, burrowing inside Sterling's forearm.

"Evenna, I'm sorry! Wake up, wake up!"

He stared at her pale face and brushed her hair out of the way. Then her shimmering lavender hair color faded to black.

This is all my fault, he realized. *I've failed Evenna. I failed Tomorak, and I am no honorable hunter.*

And he wept. As he did, a tear dripped down his scaled face onto Evenna's silver cloak, this time, soaking in the wet droplet. Banefield stirred and released a spine-chilling whinny, a horse's warning. The purple light returned along with its ominous buzz. Evenna's eyes shot open, glassy and pale.

"Evenna!"

Sterling was relieved to see the young light witch was alive. But when he looked into her eyes, he saw an emptiness, then a startling reflection of himself. Instead of a human boy looking back, it was the face of the reptile-skinned creature he had become.

CHAPTER EIGHTEEN
THE LIGHT BALL

The purple light filled the small pocket of swamp, and Evenna's eyes closed again, taking his lizardy reflection with them. He recognized her shallow breathing as a stasis—his blood magic had damaged her, but for now, she was alive, just sleeping deeply. Sterling tugged his cape over his head to shade his eyes, hoping that the purple glow wasn't a special ploy to stun the creature's victims. For now, the creature searched the swamp, slowly and methodically, and fortunately for them, on the opposite side of a thicket of trees. His mind skimmed through snapshot memories of magical creatures scrawled onto handwritten notes from his father on the topic. Fairies used glow magic, but he couldn't discount wood sprites.

He loaded Evenna's limp body into his arms quickly and listened for his horse, who must have gotten spooked by the light and taken refuge beneath the trees.

Sterling concentrated, hoping to tune into his hunter hearing, even a fraction of his abilities. But it was no use. The world of private noises and secret sounds he'd had access to was now unreachable. He had to depend on the limited capabilities of human ears. Luckily, splashing sounds came a moment later.

Horse hooves.

"Banefield!" Sterling cried out.

A muted neigh echoed in the swamps. Sterling exhaled and trudged toward it, wading through waist-deep swamp water with Evenna in his arms. He held her above the water, but one long braid had escaped her cloak. It dragged behind them in the water, greenish moss clinging to the black plait. He was relieved when Banefield's silhouette came into view. The horse stood tall, hovering over the water as three horseshoes clicked on with water-walking enchantments. The fourth horseshoe smacked against the water, and a sizable clump of swamp sludge splattered off, and the horseshoe flickered to life with the comforting blue glow of tree gnome magic.

Soon, we'll be riding out of this place, but it may not be fast enough, Sterling worried. He glanced at Evenna's closed eyes and peaceful expression, thankful that her chest still rose and fell, even if it was slight.

Sterling's hood caught on a hanging vine and slid off his head. At the first sight of Sterling's reptilian face, Banefield reared up as if to fight an enemy.

"Whoa, buddy, it's me! I'm just—I look different, that's all, but it's still me, I promise," he pleaded.

Banefield whipped his tail, and his nostrils flared. He settled as he picked up the familiar scent of his rider, but he still shied away as Sterling took a step closer.

"We need to get out of the swamp. We have to try to save Evenna," Sterling said as calmly as he could, meeting the animal's panicked eyes as a tinge of purple light peeked through the swamp trees. Banefield's ears flicked, and he tentatively stretched his nose toward Evenna. Sterling took advantage of the confusion and secured Evenna in the saddle, then climbed on behind her.

"The elves are her only hope for healing," Sterling said somberly. "Maybe witches and witch hunters can only be enemies. Even if my quest was cursed from the beginning, I've come too far to give up now."

Purple light neared the edge of the thicket and would surely detect them once it turned the corner.

He reached out to pet Banefield's mane for good luck, but the horse flinched at his touch.

"I don't blame you. I'd fear me too. But we have to go now—there's no time," Sterling muttered, his gray eyes storming.

They galloped through the Swamplands.

With the eerie purple glow disappearing behind them, their luck seemed to return. They rode through the heart of the swamp without a venomous fly in sight and soon approached the southernmost edge.

"This is where we leave the Swamplands behind," Sterling confirmed. The Elvish symbols on his arms glowed brighter. "The Sea of Griee will take us to the Hills of Bryght—to the Pearl Castle, the home of the elves."

Banefield released a snort of agreement, and his horseshoes left blue sparks as he charged over the cold seawater, his limp nearly forgotten as he plowed through the final stretch. He found comfort in the familiar voice from the saddle, and despite their dire circumstances, there was an underlying flicker of adventure and calmness that washed over the rider and his horse.

The castle was a good distance away, but Banefield's enchanted shoes gave them an advantage. Beneath dark skies, they crossed the sea with lightning speed. Saltwater beads sprayed against Sterling's scaled face, the only normal feeling he'd felt since his entire body had grown snake scales. It felt good.

It was only a matter of time before the glowing Pearl Castle would light the darkness, leading them to its gates like an iridescent beacon.

Sterling glanced down at Evenna, slung in a slouched position. Her thick braid loosened and toppled to the side, exposing the mark on her neck. It could've passed for a burn mark. But upon closer examination, there was no mistaking the telltale hunter's arrow shape—the mark of a witch hunter's attack upon a witch.

Suddenly, Evenna's metallic braid tie gleamed with purple light.

No. It's not possible for anything to track our scent over seawater.

Sterling's blood, instead of roaring inside his veins in attack mode, did nothing. Worse, his veins went numb and cool when he pressed his scaly palm against his wrist.

No, no! Please don't reverse—don't go cold. Hold on—we can make it to the elves. Just hold on a little longer!

Banefield raced away from the light, but it followed. One of his hooves sparked as it collided with an ocean rock. Banefield gritted his teeth, but he was spent. He tried to neigh but instead gasped for breath. Sterling glanced at the horse's hind leg and gulped at the line of sickly green mucus oozing from under the bandage.

"It's okay, Banefield. You were amazing, and we couldn't have made it this far without you. Stop here," Sterling said, patting the horse's side as they stopped and hovered over the seawater. Banefield sighed and leaned away from his injured leg, keeping his weight off of it.

Sterling tugged on a rein to turn around and face the persistent light as it hovered toward them. Something about it was familiar, but with his senses dulled, he couldn't be sure. So far, it had tracked them but caused no harm. In his experience, this was either a curious creature or a predator carefully biding time for the most opportune moment to attack.

"Your tracking skills are impressive!" Sterling half shouted at the purple-and-pink sphere. He figured he'd state the obvious because he really had no other plan, and his dulled sense of smell could make out nothing but the smell of seawater and a whiff of the putrid puss oozing from Banefield's leg. They could not run any longer.

The swamp sludge is in his blood—the wound is infected. I should have rewrapped his leg. Sterling realized his error.

The ball of light floated closer then stopped directly above them.

That's no venomous fly, he thought as he brandished his dagger.

"I don't want to fight you, but I will," Sterling yelled. He pulled himself to a crouch on the saddle and tapped Banefield with the signal to duck his head. As the purple thing dipped closer, Sterling tensed and leaped, dagger first. For a second as he shot through the salty air, he locked eyes with the light ball. And everything went black.

CHAPTER NINETEEN
SHIMMERING WINGS

Sterling's eyes shot open. It was still dark, but his body was illuminated by a purple glow. His rain-soaked boots dangled above round masses cloaked in shadow, and his body hung in the air. Yet he was not falling. The wind was tame, and he had a bird's-eye view of perfectly sculpted mounds. As his vision cleared, a glimmer of lavender sparkled as it weaved around the mounds.

Elvish roads—I'm flying over the Hills of Bryght. I must be dreaming, he thought as his head throbbed.

"I wondered when you'd wake up, Sterling. You're just in time to see the Pearl Castle," a high-pitched voice sang.

Sterling rubbed his eyes and noticed a spherical underbelly bowing outward directly above him. It was covered in purple fuzz.

"Saja the ink fly?" he asked, suddenly recognizing

his friend. "How did you find me? Evenna and Banefield—are they okay?"

"Your horse is in good hands—dragon hands. Your honorary brother, Green, came with me when I told him what I'd seen. He's taking Banefield to the Alin for healing. Swamp infection can be tricky to cure. What happened to your girlfriend here? She doesn't look good, Sterl," she delicately explained.

"She's not my..." Sterling replied as he caught a glimpse of Evenna's body dangling in one of Saja's spare legs. Guilt crept into his throat, and he found he didn't have the strength to admit what he'd done.

"Thank you, Saja. I don't know how you found me, especially looking the way I do now," he said as a tear burned in the corner of his eye.

"Humans care too much about looking human. Animals, insects—we don't care about appearance unless it helps us survive. Besides, you'll be with the elves soon. Maybe they can help you both," she said, seeming to recognize his pain.

Sterling let his body go limp.

"You know, snakeskin isn't all bad," Saja declared. "It has its perks too. Like that swamp sludge you got into—your skin would be crawling with sandworms like Banefield if you didn't have it."

"I suppose that's the silver lining." Sterling grimaced. Why were there so many skin-burrowing insects? "Thanks, Saja. How did you find me?"

Saja sighed. "I was on a quest to investigate the borders of the Crystal Sea. I heard gossip of a witch in disguise on the kingdom roads. Then, I bumped into a pleasant wizard with a pack of donkeys who offered to take me to her. It turned out that the witch was with you, and the wizard had a convincing story that the witch put a spell on you—that she'd turn you into a snake unless we destroyed her. I was going to help him—I thought I was helping you! But then I realized the wizard had it wrong."

"That was you in the swamp! The explosion." Sterling pieced it all together.

"I'm sorry, Sterling. As I said, the wizard was very convincing, and the girl *was* a witch. When you pulled your family dagger, I realized you were protecting her. So I turned my ink flash away in time to spare her," Saja explained. "Banefield didn't even put up a fight when Green scooped him up. I was meant to find you both—I hope the elves can save your girlfriend," she thought aloud, swooping down toward the iridescent castle of the elves.

Sterling's forearms glowed bright like starlight as they pulled toward the castle. The symbols were the only thing left on his body that he recognized anymore.

Near the narrow solitary bridge that led to the castle's entrance, Saja placed Sterling and Evenna onto the glowing stones as she hovered in the night air.

"Please stay?" Sterling asked, watching her wings flutter as she prepared to take flight. One shimmered purple and the other, a gift from Green the Story

Dragon, a teal green. He'd forgotten how enchanting Saja looked.

"I'm sorry, Sterl. If my quest was not dire, you know I'd stay," Saja said, glancing at the Elvish castle. "Alins across Everen are expecting me, and I've already been gone too long. Stay here and heal—there are turbulent times ahead and you will need your strength."

Saja's body grew to three times its normal size and pulsed a soft purple-pink glow. "Be careful with the witch girl—whatever she is to you, she carries great power, and that can be a dangerous thing," she whispered.

Before Sterling could speak, the ink fly vanished, leaving behind a spherical dust formation that slowly drifted to the ground.

With Saja's words lingering in his mind and her purple dust smeared into the stone pathway, Sterling lifted a colorless Evenna into his arms. Her pulse had slowed to a half beat—something hunters knew all too well. It was the time just before life left the body. Sterling ran. He focused only on the castle gates as ancient Elvish whispers filled his ears.

CHAPTER TWENTY
THE GATE GUARDS

Sterling barreled toward two particularly tall guards. Both stood in front of the Pearl Castle entrance, cloaked in pristine white cloth with thick hoods concealing their faces. Sterling collapsed onto his knees before them, chest heaving. The snakeskin had tightened around his ribcage and was squeezing the breath from his lungs. He raised his arms, holding up Evenna's still form.

"Help us, please," Sterling's words rang out in the cool, night air. His voice quivered like a child lost in the woods as his blood flowed cold as ice in his veins.

But the guards stood unmoving and soundless.

Think, Fierce. The Acreedian dragon feathers!

"Look!" he shouted to gain the guards' attention. In a panic, he freed one arm and waved it.

Once they see the symbols, they'll let us in.

But again, his efforts were ignored.

"I don't understand. The Elvish markings—they

were just here!" Sterling stared in horror at the plain black glossy scales along his wrist. He raised the other but it had suffered the same fate.

"I'm sorry, Evenna," he whimpered. His hand slid beneath her frail body. Holding her brought him comfort, and he hoped somehow she felt it too.

But then, Sterling's wrists narrowed and twisted. His arms mutated into serpent-like appendages, giving him a half-monster, half-human appearance. His fingers curled into snake tails and merged. He lost his grip, and Evenna thumped against the hard ground. The outline of her body faded into a shadow against the moonlight glow of the stones beneath her.

Sterling's eyes darted around with panic. He wished Saja were still with him. If this was the end of him, he yearned to be whisked back home to Bren to say goodbye to his uncle, his Alin, and his horse.

But Saja was nowhere to be seen—probably miles away by now.

One guard turned a shrouded face toward Sterling. Beneath the thick hood, a pair of teal eyes gleamed against the darkness. Only the Elvish race had eyes this color that he found alluring and terrifying at the same time.

Suddenly, a curved blade with engraved symbols pressed against Sterling's slithering arms, pinning them down. Despite their hideous appearance, Sterling couldn't bear to lose them. His heart thumped against his ribcage, and his throat was as dry as the desert dunes.

"Please. I am no threat. I've come for healing—my arms—the scales—it's a witch's curs-s-s," Sterling sputtered as his tongue split at the tip, becoming glossy black and forked.

He knew what was happening but was powerless to stop it.

"I've seen enough. Let's put him out of his misery," one guard said.

"Wait," the other guard interrupted. She knelt next to the wild, flopping snake arms. Instead of drawing her sword or gasping in terror (which would have been reasonable), she tapped on her partner's blade with three slender fingers.

The guard with the sword raised the blade slightly, allowing one of Sterling's flailing appendages to slither free, while the guard next to him spoke aloud in Elvish. The fluent, melodic flow of their foreign language calmed him. The freed serpent arm stopped writhing and tilted its tipped end toward the guard, then slithered obediently into her cupped hands. Her Elvish skin was cool to the touch and sent a feeling of peace radiating throughout his body. His heartbeat returned to a normal rhythm.

Swallowing, then taking a deep breath, he concentrated on calming his other serpent arm. It, too, became relaxed.

The guard, now at eye level with Sterling, stared into his eyes, then inspected his midnight scales.

"The boy has Elvish markings. They are cloaked in shadow form now," she confirmed.

"Yes-s-s," Sterling whimpered and hissed all at once.

"Save your energy, hunter. Stay calm. It's the only way to slow the curse," she said in a stern, motherly tone.

The other guard audibly huffed. "They could be false—just a witch's illusion. We must not let them enter. They could be spies from the other side."

The female guard closed her eyes, knitting her teal eyebrows. She whispered in a dialect more ancient than anything Sterling had heard before. A melody of guttural notes echoed through the night air as if a giant were striking an enormous set of hollow wooden tubes. Then, the scales on his hands (or where his hands used to be) interlocked and clicked out of place, revealing the symbols glowing a pale shade of starlight.

"They are no illusion. These are our markings. Acreedian dragon feathers, one on each arm. He is a welcome guest among us. Only Queen Clarelle could have gifted a tattoo with ink made from Elvish starlight. You know this, Macagh."

Sterling tried to lock eyes with the first guard. If he could look into his eyes, maybe he would see enough human worth saving.

The male guard shook his hooded head and turned away. "Maybe he was once an honored friend, but look at him now. He got himself cursed. The snakeskin has taken over. There won't be much left of him by morning—not any human parts, anyway. And the witch is on her deathbed. The mark on her neck is a fatal blow—hunter's sting. It seems these two tried to kill each other and now they have regrets. Their quarrels are of no concern to the elves," he said.

"Queen Clarelle can cure the hunter and maybe the young witch too, if we hurry!" the female guard protested.

"We cannot risk the safety of our home for two mortal lives—not in these times. There is too much at stake for our kind. You know this, Strellian," he said.

The guard Strellian tossed her hood back and stood with her face inches from the guard Macagh. A flash came from Strellian's eyes, and the male guard's shoulders dipped in response.

"I know how you feel about mortals," he said gently, "but it's not a time to take unnecessary risks—not until we know why the fog has breached more of Everen's borders. War is certainly coming. These two could be spies sent by the dark elves."

"And if they're not? Nobody knows why the fog has come. It doesn't mean we cannot help those in need. How would the queen react if she hears an honored friend died at our feet and we did nothing to aid him? He is a friend asking for healing, and we cannot deny him the alliance he's been promised. If we aren't clever enough to see the truth, we will never be more than gate guards. This is our chance to prove that we can be more."

"He is only losing his human form, Strellian, not his life. Besides, he's a feisty one. He'll make a fine serpent," Macagh retorted. Behind the shadow of his hood, Sterling was sure the guard smirked at his misfortune.

"Macagh, you are entitled to your destiny. And I am entitled to mine," she whispered as she lowered her face to Sterling's.

"Come, hunter, this may be the most painful thing you've ever done. Best to get it out of the way."

Sterling instinctively flicked his new tongue into the air and caught a burst of saltiness. He hadn't noticed the tears streaming down his reptilian face. In seconds, he was showered in a pulsing glow of crimson light, and the world enlarged in every way, then darkened. Muscles shifted and bones morphed. From his new position mere inches from the ground, he had never felt so afraid.

CHAPTER TWENTY-ONE
A SERPENT'S VIEW

T he sound of metal clinking against metal rattled inside Sterling's suddenly tiny skull, followed by a melodic thumping.

Footsteps and an Elvish blade tapping against a belt link, Sterling figured as his reptilian eyes opened for the first time.

He was tucked away in the guard's cloak, buried in a deep pocket that swayed as the guard walked with urgency. Despite being transformed into a serpent, he could think clearly and in human words. A wave of control washed over his smooth black scales as he became attuned to his alert senses. After his hunter abilities had diminished, he'd lost his link with the physical world around him. His senses were different, but the connection was reborn.

He crept his elongated, limbless body toward a crease of crisp white light overhead. His underbelly scales clicked into motion, allowing him to climb up the thick cloth, and he peeked out from the pocket. With a flick of his tongue, he tasted through the air the minerals that had hardened beneath the castle's sea-pearl surfaces. The corridor had the same shape as he recalled from his first time inside the castle. The halls arched to a high point in the middle that easily accommodated the height of the Elvish race. Though, something was different this time. The colors blended into one another, a backdrop of vibrant blue and violet with blobs of yellow outlined in orange. His new serpent sight was unpleasant, but it worked.

Then, a second flick of his tongue detected a woodsy scent. It was oak tree innards with a pinch of bark mold and traces of horsehair. Using his new thermal detection ability, he cricked his slender neck to spy a yellow outline of a body slumped over the guard's arm. The mass was a collection of orange and yellow smears with specks of red mostly at the eyes, throat, and mouth. Even slung upside down and through serpent eyes, he knew it was Evenna. He allowed his muscles to relax, thankful that she was still alive.

The swaying footsteps stopped as they arrived at an exceptionally tall set of doors with ornate star-and-moon carvings. A standing figure, a yellowish mass with blue pointed ears, stood with the hilt of a sword peeking from behind their shoulder. Sterling slipped back below the cloak pocket, hoping that he hadn't been spotted.

Murmurs of Elvish words bounced off the

smooth, pearl walls, and vibrations tickled his scales. One of the voices was Strellian's, but her words were garbled as if she were underwater. The second voice was deep, masculine, and equally unclear. Perhaps snakes couldn't interpret nonreptile languages. The voices rose to shouting, and two spots behind his eyes throbbed as if they would burst. Worse, he had no hands to cover them. He dove deep into his pocket, trying to escape the unbearable noise. His tail instinctively slid over his head until silence came.

Whatever Strellian's argument was, it was convincing enough to allow them passage into the queen's chambers. Sterling instantly recognized the voice of Queen Clarelle. It was eloquent and singular, bold but gentle. He bolted to catch a glimpse of the Elvish queen. Her chambers were draped in shadows deep as night except where teardrop-shaped moon rock hung from the ceiling, casting a bright white glow. They glowed from their cores, giving enough light for the elves to see. But they quickly overwhelmed Sterling's reptilian eyes, so he took to darting his gaze into the shadows.

Vine-wrapped columns shimmered with occasional bursts of fairy glitter and puffs from bubble flowers. A trickling waterfall poured from above into a deep pool that twirled inside a cluster of clear tubes, splashing into one of a dozen water sculptures. Each unique sculpture was adorned with wide flower pads composed of powder-blue petals surrounding starlight centers. Somehow, Sterling could see the flowers in their true colors. But Elvish magic was ancient and secluded from outsiders, so oddities were to be expected within a castle as magical as this one.

Moon fairies hummed a familiar tune. Sterling uncoiled himself completely and stretched his neck higher toward the fairies. Everything here was serene, as usual. Everything except the fairies. They were tense. Pointy-tipped wings fluttered as fairies the size of a human hand squeezed burnt red juice from fire beetles into glass bottles. More sets of winged workers swooped down to cork the full bottles and stack them into assorted transport containers.

Strellian murmured something that Sterling assumed was a respectful apology.

"Something is dire to you, Strellian. Show me what it is," Queen Clarelle said, still nowhere in sight, though her words were perfectly clear to his reptilian ears.

Strellian emitted more underwater sounds in reply, then rummaged in her cloak. Sterling flinched as she grasped his slender body in both hands and placed him on a flat surface. Instantly, a trio of translucent spheres, each the size of a watermelon, floated toward him.

Seeing spheres, he realized, but his reflexes were faster than his logic. His tail tucked into a tight spiral so that his limbless body looked like a serpent pyramid. Spontaneously, his jaw widened, and he let out a hiss. The spheres darted toward him anyway. He catapulted into the air, landing headfirst into an open palm adorned with thick silver-banded rings. Burning venom shot into his fangs, and there was no thinking, only fear and the overpowering desire to survive.

As he darted forward to strike everything in his path, his serpent body froze in midair, as if time had stopped. It was then that a pair of glowing lavender eyes pierced through him with the coolness of a skilled hunter delivering a fatal blow.

CHAPTER TWENTY-TWO
SERPENT'S CHOICE

"I would recognize the storm of bravery in those eyes in any form you take. Yet you are not yourself, Sterling Fierce. You have come to the right place. Much is possible in the realm of elves," Queen Clarelle said, tilting her head as she peered deeper into his eyes. She read his recent past and understood his dire circumstances.

The burning sensation dissipated from his fangs as exhaustion washed over him, although he remained frozen in midair, unable to do more than twitch his tail.

Strellian's distorted words rumbled nearby, lulling him into a deeper state of relaxation. It was only when he made out the word "witch" that his reptilian mind regained a sense of worry for his friend. *Evenna*, he suddenly remembered. How had he forgotten about her?

"Sterling, you have a choice to make. It is not an

easy one, but you must decide now before any more time slips away. I can extract the curse and restore you to your human form with hunter abilities intact. Though, I'm afraid the light witch will not survive the full extraction. She intertwined part of her life force into the curse, a common mistake for a young witch."

She concocted a mixture in a bowl, scraping the bottom with a crystal-tipped spoon.

A thousand tiny braids cascaded down her back like a magnificent teal waterfall of hair, adorned with metallic trinkets. Unraveling one of the shimmery gold trinkets from one of her braids, she dropped it into the bowl with a loud clunk.

"Her emotions ran too deep. Did you have a connection with this witch before, Sterling?" Queen Clarelle asked, tossing another hair trinket into the bowl. This time, the concoction popped with a splash of sparkles.

"Not ex-x-xactly," a hiss of words escaped his clenched jaw. To his surprise and delight, human speech returned. "It's-s-s complicated-d, Your Majesty, but I cannot let Evenna come to harm-s-s."

"I see. Then we have one other option. Your body can be healed, returning to human form, but part of the curse would remain. This would allow Evenna to live, but your blood magic may suffer beyond repair or be lost altogether."

The words stung to his core. Being a witch hunter was who he was—who he'd become. Who was he without his abilities?

"Do it-t. Pleas-s-s-e," he begged, pushing selfish thoughts to the corner of his mind.

Queen Clarelle's eyes flashed, summoning a lavender-colored mist from the bowl. It weaved through the air and sprinkled over Sterling, releasing him from his stonelike state. His slender body dropped into her open palms. Her skin was flawless periwinkle and as soft as honey soap.

Queen Clarelle patted his top scales.

"It is time. You will feel pain, but that is to be expected as the curse leaves your body," she explained, motioning toward a seeing sphere with an opening just his size.

Sterling bobbed his head and flicked his forked tongue nervously as he stared at the sphere's hole. The air tasted like wet stone and burnt metal. Around him, fairies left trails of glitter as they carried more bottles to the transport. Sterling tried to gulp, but snake mouths weren't made for such an action, so he slithered silently into the sphere. Despite the queen's calm demeanor, she seemed tense. He realized that the guards held the same tension, a quiver in their voices and a shifting of their eyes. And now he detected apprehension in the fairies—like the stillness of forest creatures before a storm.

The clinking of bottles and sloshing of beetle blood echoed in his ears as the sphere sealed around him. His body immediately warmed, and his scales became glossy, dripping with black slime.

Snakes don't sweat, he thought, but logic didn't

matter here. The black goo thickened, flooding the small orb. There was an awful splinter of pain as one of his scales peeled off. It was worse than the feeling of tearing off a fresh scab, and he might have screamed if snake voices were designed for such things. One by one, his scales cracked away as if giant fingers were ripping them off. He instinctively dove to the bottom of the sphere, hoping to find the hole from where he'd entered, but it had been sealed. Panic set in. There was no way out, and the sphere was nearly full of black sludge. It would be mere moments before breathable air was gone.

He wriggled his body, propelling himself back up for one last gasp. The goo plopped over his eyes, and everything went dark. A strange sensation of being pulled in opposing directions came over him. Then, a pulse shocked his body as the sphere burst open. Black muck splattered against pristine pearl floors. A golden-brown ball wrapped around bones as muscle emerged within, slowly forming skin into the shape of a recognizable human body. Human eyes widened. Two arms grew from the mass and digits extended from balled-up fists. Legs, ankles, then feet sprouted the same way.

Sterling shook his head as messy waves of chestnut brown hair sprung into place. Lashes, eyebrows, and fingernails filled in, and he swayed before giving in and letting his body crash to the ground. His nonscaly hand smeared black goop across the pearl-coated floor. He stared at his reflection in the pearly luster and recognized his own features, scars and wispy beard included. The broad jawline, sturdy nose, and full lips looked alien to him at first. But his gray eyes swirled, and he knew he'd returned.

Sterling tilted his head to catch a glimpse of Queen Clarelle tending to Evenna. The elf's lavender light mist whirled over the light witch's petite body. Her skin deepened with its natural violet tinge, and her braid pulsed teal before returning to a sullen black and white.

"As I suspected," the queen said with satisfaction. "She is not a full witch. Though, you must have noticed, my astute hunter," she said in a low voice, placing her hands over Evenna.

"I—um," he stuttered, still adjusting to his human form. A breeze skittered across his bare skin, and he realized he was only wearing a few sticky patches of black gunk.

A trio of fairies fluttered toward him, dropping a sack containing his hunter clothes and gear at his feet. They giggled as they glided back to their bottling station, and Sterling prayed that Evenna would stay asleep until he could manage to pull on his trousers.

CHAPTER TWENTY-THREE
UNEXPECTED GUESTS

S trellian skirted around the corner with a tray of assorted drinks and marble-sized nourishment cubes. Her metallic boots skidded in a patch of splattered black residue that the fairies had overlooked during their tidying up of the pearl floors. Strellian stopped in front of the hunter, who clutched his cape and dagger sheath over the middle of his body.

"You look…different," Strellian admitted, sounding less bold than before and certainly not the imposing Elvish guard persona from the castle gate. She'd removed her hood, unveiling a youthful face and wide eyes. Sterling peered at her, willing his eyes to take in detail, but he felt like he was peering through murky glass. Was this how normal humans saw the world?

Strellian's lush blond hair parted into thirds. One section spilled onto her back and the other two lay neatly over her shoulders. Her vibrant locks were wrapped in a set of some kind of white cloth ties. Something flashed on Strellian's cheek as her eye twitched. Sterling squinted to make out a patch of iridescent crystals arranged in a crescent moon shape.

"You look different too," Sterling replied before turning around and quickly pulling on a dusty set of brown pants bearing mismatched stitching. The clothes, old things of his father's he'd recently grown into, had always felt rough and manly, but Sterling frowned at the coarse fabric, surprised that the texture seemed flatter.

"Besides, the scales and fangs weren't really my style," he said, shoving his hand-me-down shirt over his brown curls. His biceps bulged as he tugged the shirt to face forward, drawing Strellian's gaze. His midnight-blue sleeves trickled with dust and sweat particles, catching on to the broadest part of his shoulders. Sterling sneezed, and black mucus droplets trickled out of his nose. He frowned as even that sensation felt numbed. When he looked up, Strellian was gazing thoughtfully at his midsection, which rippled with two distinct rows of abdominal muscles.

Strellian pointedly lifted her eyes to his. "I meant only that your eyes look more Elvish than I've seen in a human before," she clarified, clearing her throat with audible embarrassment as Sterling tucked in his shirt.

"He's not an ordinary human, Strellian." The queen's voice rang from the healing table across the room. It rose from the pearly floor over a smooth cascade of ice-colored steps.

"He's a witch hunter. The old books refer to a hunter's eyes as taking on the appearance of a bird of prey. Our guest is capable of unspeakable damage to his enemies. Even with his blood magic damaged, it is good fortune that he hunts witches and not elves," Queen Clarelle explained in a somber tone, managing to speak and weave a healing spell into Evenna at the same time.

Sterling couldn't tell if the queen had just complimented or insulted witch hunters. In any case, he wasn't a real witch hunter anymore, not without his blood magic. He felt like a fraud as he tied on his hunter's cape and stepped into his father's knee-high boots, scratched, and worn from many travels. He released a defeated sigh and forced thoughts of blood magic to the back of his mind.

Evenna's fragile body lay on an iridescent oval table. Several moon lamps had lowered as the queen worked. They seemed brighter than ever, but Sterling frowned, realizing he couldn't really see what was going on. He took a few steps closer on wobbly legs as the queen threaded a glowing strand into the side of Evenna's neck. Despite the elf's ministrations, Evenna didn't seem to have improved. Her nose and lips looked tiny and lifeless, like those of a child's toy doll, drained of color and life.

I lost control, and Evenna paid the cost. She trusted me

to protect her. I don't deserve my gifts anymore, he told himself.

More than anything, he wished for Evenna to wake (and forgive him). As if his wishes had a power of their own, her skin flashed periwinkle, then returned to her usual porcelain white with a violet undertone. Her hair brightened from black to a mix of blues as Queen Clarelle chanted a final prayer in Elvish. Evenna's entire body floated off the table a few inches before a blinding white light flashed inside her, filling the room like a silent explosion.

Sterling's eyes were slow to adjust to the darkness again, but there was a flicker of something magical as he finally focused on the scene in front of him.

One glistening bead of sweat rolled down Queen Clarelle's unblemished brow. Sterling stared at it, willing his eyes to focus on the fine details, but it was like his hunter's blood went to sleep, and the droplet faded from view with one final sparkle.

"There. Your friend has been saved. She will need rest, and the scar will remain, but she will mend. The power she has is something rare—two magical beings in one, drawing strength from both. Perhaps the magical realm is evolving in more curious ways than we could have imagined…"

Her voice trailed off as she peered at a stack of books. Cutting her piercing lavender eyes toward Sterling, she nodded. "Are you quite well, my hunter?"

"Yes, Your Majesty. That is…" he hesitated as his hunter's blood flickered then faded again. He shook his head, dismissing it. "Yes, quite well. Thank you. You've done so much for me. I do not know how to repay you, but I hope to one day. And thank you, Strellian. I am forever grateful to you too. Evenna is eternally in your debt, as am I," Sterling said in a sturdier voice. His chest tickled with tiny electric tingles, detecting witch magic once again. The queen nodded and retreated to the shadows.

Strellian finally found a place for her refreshment tray and set it down. "Take in some nourishment. There's nothing to do now but wait," she explained.

He gulped down a mug of moon juice—he tried to guess the flavors, but it all just tasted vaguely tropical—and half a dozen blue bark cakes. Strellian, ever the faithful guard, pulled out a whetstone and began polishing the curved blade of her sword.

Sterling waited for Evenna to wake and tried not to mind that the bark cakes painted his skin royal blue. With each passing moment that Evenna did not wake, he grew more anxious.

With the queen preoccupied, it felt like the right time to pry, just a little.

"Strellian, is it possible to be part Elvish and part something else?" he whispered.

"No," she said dryly, eyes fixed on an unsatisfactory inch of her blade, although to Sterling's merely human vision, it appeared perfectly sharp and deadly.

Sterling yawned, suddenly fatigued from overeating. "I've read about the possibility of an Elman. You know, half Elvish and half human. I wondered if—"

But his words were cut short when a towering male guard wearing a crimson cloak burst into the queen's chambers shouting in Elvish. Instinctively, Sterling's eyes darted to the guard's quiver of arrows. The container dripped with a deep purple residue. It was a distinct color that reminded him of dark wizards.

A tingle shot up the back of his neck.

"Take our guests to the resting quarters now," the queen hissed at Strellian before turning to the newcomer. She began questioning the red-robed guard in their native tongue, her skin morphing from periwinkle to dark teal. Fairy buzzing went silent as the guard communicated in a hurried, low growl. His Elvish was muffled, and he turned his back to Sterling and Evenna as if they were too close for his liking. Sterling couldn't hear much, but he clenched his teeth at an ancient phrase he'd read in his father's books.

Elvendra Ent Diestra.

If he remembered correctly, the words translated loosely to *Elves from the Dark Place.*

CHAPTER TWENTY-FOUR
THE MAGIC DOOR

"Come, hunter," Strellian said with hushed urgency.

"What's happening?" he asked, shaking his legs to get used to controlling them again. His boots felt like they'd been filled with sand.

"It's no concern of yours," she hissed.

"I took an oath to help protect Everen. I can help," he said.

"Out of the question. We must leave at once. Follow me—quickly!" She nodded with respect to her queen once more before scooping up Evenna and rushing to the far end of the quarters where two solid pearls met to form a shadowy corner.

He tried to catch up, but his legs were weak and readjusting to their human form. He wobbled to a stop and hunched over with a hand pressed against his thigh. He pointed questioningly behind him toward the only door he could see.

Strellian ignored him.

Unlike Sterling, her movements were graceful as she charged into a full sprint at a side wall.

Sterling blinked, and there was an arched doorway in front of her. It flickered a midnight blue and swallowed Strellian with no more trace than a few ripples.

A hidden door, he realized. *I should have known.*

It made perfect sense for a race as secretive as the elves to travel by clandestine methods. Sterling knew little about magic doors or if a human could even pass through them. But a magic door wouldn't stay open for long.

"Here goes nothing," he decided.

The sound of heavy footfalls thumped inside his skull as he tossed his body toward the shrinking doorway. He suppressed a childish grin. A thrill ran through his veins like the first time he'd jumped from a rope swing headfirst into the refreshing depths of lake water.

A burst of frigid air slammed against his chest as he passed through the magic door. He toppled out the other side with a weird tinge tugging on his hair. He realized it was static electricity, and he shook his head, trying to get used to his diminished senses. Slightly disheveled but determined, he concentrated on his new surroundings. The door had taken him to a narrow passageway drenched in shadows. The magic portal rapidly disintegrated into a pile of blue-green sand. There was no going back.

Luckily, dangling globes of moon beetles lined the

arched walls, casting a bluish glow. The dim flicker of light caught in Strellian's silvery cloak (and Evenna's) as she darted ahead. Even carrying Evenna in her arms, Strellian navigated the darkened halls with speed. Her extra height gave her an immense physical advantage, making her easily twice as fast as he could ever hope to be.

The pathway descended as it curved, and Strellian's blond locks vanished. Keeping up with her became even more daunting as the passageway split three ways.

Sterling squinted, making out a few closed doors, presumably locked, down the far-right hall.

"Everen's ghosts. Where did she go?"

From the left hallway, a door slammed. He crept in that direction, clenching his dagger hilt just in case.

"Fierce, in here."

He approached a recessed doorway and saw the shadowed door was slightly ajar. It was carved with fairy markings resembling glowing healing stones and creaked as he swung it open. Inside, the walls diverged and stretched to form a round room carpeted with living clover. He breathed in deeply, catching a sweet aroma that he felt he should have been able to identify. Watering pots painted in pastels hung in the shape of a petaled flower. Honey pods dangled from potted lavender, and a myriad of other herbs and flowers sprouted in a floating garden. The ceiling was made of pale pearls noticeably less grand compared to others in the castle. From the look of the place, it was occupied and run by a network of healing fairies and not elves at all.

No fairies were visible as he stepped into the room. Sterling assumed they were away handling bottling chores.

But they could be hiding just out of sight and my human eyes would never notice, he thought ruefully.

The space was modest, about the size of his home in Bren but with a handful of cloud beds and a wall with a dozen fairy nooks. The resting clouds hovered off the lush green clover floor, all empty except for the one where Evenna slept. Sterling collapsed into his own cloud. His eyelids drooped as he stared at Evenna's less pale cheeks and ocean-blue lashes. A calmness washed over him for the first time in days, and he was happy that she was healed.

"There is a closeness you share with this witch," Strellian said, securing a handful of herbs to her belt pouches before cloaking herself beneath her velvety hood.

Sterling furrowed his brow in response and cut his gaze to Strellian, realizing he'd forgotten she was still in the room.

"I made a promise to her grandfather to bring her home safely. Hunter's duty," he said.

"I've lived a thousand lifetimes, Sterling Fierce, but I don't need even one moon's passing to see your bond with her. It's no concern of mine. Well, I must leave now. The fairies will tend to you," she said, her teal eyes flashing under her hood one last time before she passed the threshold.

Sterling was silent. He bit his lip, wishing he knew what the Elvish guard had told the queen. If he knew the danger, he might be able to help.

"Stay here, hunter. And stay safe. That is the best way to aid us now," Strellian whispered as if she'd read his thoughts. Then she was gone.

CHAPTER TWENTY-FIVE
SNOOPING FOR SECRETS

Sterling awoke to the sound of metal boots marching outside the healing quarters—hundreds of them. He blinked through the hazy air at the pearly ceiling and rubbed his eyes. The view did not clear up. He sighed. He'd just have to get used to not having hunter's blood for now.

Once the precisely timed footsteps dulled to a hum, Sterling unlatched the door and peered down the hallway. The elves had gone, but something seemed wrong. He strained his ears, but all he could hear was his own nervous breathing.

Witch hunter... an unfamiliar voice whispered. The sound was unlike anything he had heard before.

"Sterling? Is that you?" Evenna called behind him.

"Evenna!" Sterling sighed with relief. He didn't want to turn his back on the hallway and the whispering voice. But he stuck his head out once more, and there was no further sign of it.

"How are you feeling?" he asked, turning his attention toward her.

She rubbed a new raised scar on her neck.

"I think I'm okay. Where are we? What happened in the swamp?" she asked.

Sterling explained everything to her—well, almost everything. His eyes swirled wildly with threads of gray as he skipped over the part when he'd lost his blood magic.

"They seem to be preparing for war or something," he finished. "But no one will tell me anything. All I know is there's a mysterious fog."

Evenna's forehead creased, creating delicate wrinkles. Sterling nearly reached out to smooth them but stopped himself as his ears burned. Evenna didn't seem to notice.

"But what was whispering in the hall? You said it knew you."

His gut clenched. He couldn't be sure, his senses still feeling scrambled, but the whisper tugged at him.

"It definitely wasn't a witch," he said, then realized it might have been. He'd only felt one tug of witch-hunter magic, and he couldn't be sure it would come back if he needed it.

"It was powerful as a witch?" Evenna's eyes were wide. "Do you think the queen knows?"

"I don't know. It might not be anything." Even as he said it, he knew that couldn't be true. "Maybe we should check it out just in case."

Evenna nodded and swung her legs over the edge of her cloud bed. She stood, and Sterling found he'd reached a hand out, ready to steady her if she were still weak, but she was as graceful as ever. She glanced at his outstretched hand, and before he could abashedly pull it back, she tucked her little hand into his elbow as if he were a knight and she a lady.

His heart gave a wild thump, but this wasn't any witch-hunter magic.

He escorted her to the elf-sized door, and together, they crept down the spiraled passageway.

"There," he whispered. Something cast a flicker of yellow light against one of the curved pearl walls.

"Where?" Evenna asked, craning her neck. Sterling hurried forward, gesturing. The light reflected off the iridescent pearl walls, but as they rounded the corner, there was no sign of a candle or light sphere. Yet the flickers of light kept dancing as if a torchbearer were just around the next bend.

Evenna tugged at his arm. "I don't see anything."

He turned toward her. "Nothing?" He gestured toward the warm flicker. Even without the hazy glow, he could feel something powerful tugging at him. This wasn't witch-hunting, nor was it the combination of his enhanced senses. He closed his eyes, and sure enough, there was still a tug of power. Did he have another kind of magic he'd never noticed because his powerful blood had covered it up? The thought filled him with an unexpected hope.

"Can you still see it?" Evenna whispered.

He opened his eyes, but he didn't need to. He could sense it. "Yes, this way."

They followed the light through a few more twists and around another sharp corner.

"Is the light moving?" she asked under her breath. "Do you think it's an Elvish enchantment? They like illusions."

Sterling frowned. So much for his hidden magic theory. But until they found the source, they couldn't know for sure.

"It can't be much farther."

Finally, they reached a door. It was blocked by a stack of storage spheres made of blue bark wood.

"In there?" Evenna said, pulling her warm hand off his arm, making his skin feel suddenly cold in its absence. "How would light even get past these containers, much less through that door?"

Sterling was already rolling the storage spheres aside. They were heavier than they looked.

When the last obstacle was pushed out of the way, Sterling placed his palm against the heavy stone door.

"Very curious—it's Grunne stone. This is a sacred rock used to defend entire cities. They wouldn't use this if it weren't guarding something powerful or dangerous—maybe both," Sterling said, arching his brows with restrained excitement. The door opened easily and silently, revealing a darkened room lined with the same sacred stone.

"I'm not sure about this, Sterling. Maybe we shouldn't meddle. If the elves found us snooping around..."

"We'll be in and out, hunter's promise. Besides, we owe the elves—they saved us both," he replied in his best pecan salesman voice.

Evenna cleared her throat and ducked under his arm, which still held the stone door ajar.

Inside was a magnificent laboratory. Barrels of yellow, blue, and red liquid bubbled as the colorful mixtures swam upward into hanging ceiling tubes. Thousands of bright loops wiggled above his head.

"Is this the light?" Evenna gestured at a golden glow underneath a bubbling cauldron.

"This looks just like the potion wizard's!" Sterling said with a smile. He'd have to tell Evenna the whole story later. "But no..." The power source still tugged at him, and it wasn't leading toward the cauldron.

Evenna darted to a shelving system with different types of eggs stored in rows of see-through drawers. Elvish symbols marked each row, all unique.

"These eggs are warm!" she whispered with enthusiasm, tracing her fingertips over a thick, spotted egg.

"Wait—don't disturb them. We don't know what's inside," Sterling warned. "Hunters don't trust creature hatchlings of any size. It's not the hatchling we worry about—it's the parents."

"Oh, I didn't realize," she admitted. "I just hoped it was something fluffy and adorable."

"Not likely," Sterling whispered as he inspected the symbols painted on the drawers. "I don't recognize the markings, but they're all being incubated to hatch. Wait, this can't be…" Sterling stopped dead in his tracks near a row of swirl-patterned eggs.

Evenna rushed toward him.

"You know what they are! What are they?" she asked, probing him with wide eyes.

"It's nothing," Sterling muttered, hurrying across to the other side of the room only to bump into Evenna, who was somehow in front of him again.

"What are you not telling me?" she scolded.

"How'd you do that?" Sterling gasped.

"Do what?" she snapped.

"You just appeared all the way across the room—like magic. You mean to tell me you have no idea how you did that?"

"That's right." Evenna sighed in frustration.

It seemed unlikely, but Evenna also didn't seem like she was lying.

"Fine, just leave the eggs alone and help me look for any unusual source of light or heat, or something," he requested.

Evenna meandered down the next row of oddities and tapped on glass containers filled with assorted crystals. Each one pulsed a dull glow in response. Sterling wanted to lecture her about meddling with magic ingredients, but it had been his idea to come investigate in the first place. He tried to focus on finding whatever had called to him—it was here somewhere. Then, his ears popped, and he was suddenly aware of a high-pitched tone from an upper shelf. He jumped back as the noise continued. Were those his hunter reflexes finally returning?

CHAPTER TWENTY-SIX

BROKEN GLASS AND OTHER CURIOUS THINGS

"Are you doing that?" he asked Evenna, plugging his ears.

But she didn't seem to hear any of the commotion; she was quietly building a miniature castle on a nearby table with a mix of crystal dust and magnetic beads.

Meanwhile, containers on the shelves nearby began to rattle, and the clinking of glass buzzed in Sterling's mind.

It felt like his hunter's hearing fought against the remains of the curse inside his body, tiny pins poking inside his veins.

Stop, he commanded his blood, and it complied.

A shadow caught his eye, and he climbed the shelves to get a better look. Removing a handful of dusty books, he unearthed a glowing globe the size of a bear cub. His senses tingled, and he relaxed.

"I found the light source! It must've had an energy

spike earlier. It's a star, shrunk down to a sliver of its original size. But it's just as powerful. I've never seen anything like it outside of paintings and books," Sterling said, rattling off more star facts.

"It's called a star gem. Even my elders have never seen one—very rare," Evenna confessed, tilting her head toward the gleaming ball of light. "But stars don't whisper people's names, Sterling."

"Oh, no, I guess not." Something still tugged at him, and he scanned the shelves. "We might have to check out the rest of the castle. There's nothing else here except potion bottles and healing herbs." He extended his foot to climb down the shelf, but when he put his weight down, his boot slipped in a powdery residue.

His arms flailed, and he managed to push off against the shelf to turn in the air. He tucked his legs under his body and landed catlike on all fours.

"That was close!" he exclaimed, rising from his crouch. But the sound of breaking glass echoed across the laboratory.

"You woke something up—something bad!" Evenna cried out, pointing at purple smoke seeping from a pile of crushed glass.

It rose, forming the head and shoulders of something resembling an Elvish warrior. Smoky fog crackled with electric snaps as the ghostlike warrior aimed a set of curved swords at Sterling. The elf's eyes were empty black holes—the same eyes as the terrifying night trolls. Vaporous swords struck through the air, cutting fast, inches from Sterling's throat, and he waved his flaming dagger at the black-eyed attacker. The imposing figure didn't flinch at Sterling's fiery blade. It was his only weapon, and it would not be enough.

"I don't have time to explain, but my blood magic won't help us. Evenna, you have to use your magic!" Sterling yelled as he crouched into a defensive stance and gripped his dagger.

A beam of light magic slapped the curved swords back, but the dark being recovered quickly, taking a second shot at slicing off Sterling's head. This time, a whip of white light cut through the air as Evenna hurled a stronger dose of magic. The purple shadow shook off the white whip, tearing it in two before advancing again at Sterling. Both swords came at Sterling's neck in an X pattern, an old swordsman's technique used to separate the head from the body in one clean scissor slice. This was a barbaric move, even among hunters.

Sterling kept his flaming dagger up, blocking and defending as best as he could without his blood magic. His hearing decided to take a little vacation as white light collided with his blade. His dagger seemed to grow as it became engulfed in white flame.

He had no time to marvel at the fiery anomaly that transformed his blade. The shadowy attacker's swords were once again inches from his throat. Sterling ducked, then charged into the warrior's center, plunging his new white-hot dagger where any normal being's heart should be. The tip of Sterling's blade burst through its misty purple chest, and the fog disintegrated into blackened dust at Sterling's boots.

Evenna crumpled to her knees. Her forehead and back were drenched with sweat. Her magic was depleted, and it would take time to restore her energy after launching such a powerful spell.

"Why did it attack us? Why's your blood magic gone?" she panted.

"I don't know, but our purple attacker...the fog that everyone's worried about—it's all related," he huffed, wiping sweat from his brow, and inspecting his dagger. Somehow, Evenna's magic had intertwined with the dragon magic within his blade—a super weapon.

"I can manage the truth—all of it this time," she replied, twisting her head to inspect the white-flamed dagger.

Sterling's shoulders drooped.

"Okay, here's what I think. The fog is a magical weapon used by dark elves—the elves of Everen must've intercepted some of it and locked it in here. We're all in grave danger when an army of those fog elves attack—and I suspect many know it," he said, taking a pause to chug water out of a nearby herb-watering container. "And your light magic mixed with the dragon fire in my dagger—I'm able to destroy dark elves' magic with it. I believe it's my destiny to fight against them. This quest—me and you—it was all meant to happen like this."

"But you lost your blood magic? How?" she demanded.

After a long pause, he continued, "The queen couldn't destroy the curse in me, not all of it, without killing you too. So she left part of it behind, and my blood magic is lost to it."

Evenna sat in silence, her veins glowing in places.

"How could you forgive me? The serpent curse—your lost blood magic is because of me."

Sterling shook his head. "No, Evenna. You didn't know any better when you touched my hand—I didn't know either. I'm the one who almost killed you in the swamp. For days, I watched you die, and *that* was my fault alone. I didn't control my power, and I don't deserve blood magic if I can't protect the ones I care about from it."

Evenna's face suddenly seemed inches from his own, the warmth of her breath against his cheek. The sides of his neck tingled, making him lightheaded like the time he'd drunk his father's ale.

The bottles on the shelves rattled softly. Sterling detected minuscule vibrations, but it was a clear warning to leave before more magical curiosities were invoked.

"We need to get proof of the dark elves to the Alin—a sample for him to study. He'll know what to do," he said, distancing himself and pocketing a small bottle of purple fog.

Evenna stood and smoothed out the creases in her

velvety cloak, retightening the plush silk rope across her shoulders.

"How can we leave this castle? It's heavily guarded, and we don't have a horse even if we can escape unnoticed," Evenna asked with her usual panicked expression.

"Leave that to me and an old family friend," Sterling announced with a grin.

CHAPTER TWENTY-SEVEN
A WAY OUT

Treading lightly through hidden passageways and skittering along arched tunnels, Sterling and Evenna reached the castle's top floor. From the soaring heights of the castle's rooftop, the domed roofs below were astounding. Sterling imagined this was what the ocean floor would look like if sea pearls expanded to enormous proportions. He peered at the gleaming city below, but something was wrong. Where were all the citizens? The whole place seemed deserted. His hunter's vision sharpened, and he caught the barest flicker of purple. His spine chilled at the color. Dark elves couldn't have infiltrated the castle already, could they? He clutched the bottle in his pocket. They needed to get back to the Alin and find some answers fast.

Neither Sterling nor Evenna' had detected the seeing sphere approaching from behind. Tingles shot from his elbow to fingertips, and he whirled. Inches from his waist, the sphere scanned his dagger. His childish fear of being sucked into a seeing sphere floated through his thoughts no matter how much he told himself that was impossible.

"Welcome back to our castle, hunter from Bren," the sphere said in a faint whisper that caught in the wind, nearly carried away before he could make out the words.

Sterling cleared his throat and thanked the sphere with a respectful bow. It floated calmly toward Evenna, then sidled next to her at eye level.

"Rare—very rare, indeed. The lost daughter of two worlds. It is not safe for you in these times, Evenna, daughter of Ohann."

Evenna's face went stark white.

"What is this thing? How does it know me?" Evenna whimpered. She grasped for the sphere as it shrunk to the size of a tiny soap bubble, then popped.

"You can't take everything a seeing sphere says to heart. Besides, they get mortals mixed up all the time. C'mon, we have a dragon to find," Sterling said, hoping to distract Evenna while committing the sphere's words to his memory.

"Dragon?! No—no. No dragons," she said, twitching her head nervously in a gesture Sterling took to be refusal. He instantly regretted giving away his plan. Who would have thought a witch would be afraid of a dragon?

"Acreedians are a special breed. Very wise and loyal. Besides, if we want to get to your grandfather quickly, this is our only choice. Try not to be nervous, please. They'll get jumpy if we don't stay calm. Just think of them as winged horses," Sterling said convincingly and gave Evenna's cloak a playful tug. She began to float a few inches and fought to control her panic.

"Fine. But I don't want to ever meet another one of those talking bubbles," she said, her feet landing on the parapet once more. She hesitantly followed Sterling uphill on a path that weaved through dozens of squatly towers. Slipping into a dark cave, unnoticed, they entered a flat landing. Ropes hung just out of reach, and pale moon globes emitted a peaceful glow bright enough to illuminate a few feet around them.

"Alright, jump as high as you can and pull one of the ropes. It'll take you to the dragon fields." Sterling instructed, immediately taking his own advice.

"Sterling!" Evenna's voice called into the hollow shaft as his boots spun up and out of sight.

Above the dragon stalls, Sterling's mood suddenly darkened. His mind scrambled at the sight of thousands of Acreedians, all with matching turquoise fur coats and broad wings covered in cloud-white feathers. There were more dragons than he could have imagined. Normally, he'd have been impressed by the Elvish illusion enchantments hiding the awe-inspiring dragon fleet. Instead, a sense of panic rippled in his chest.

"I'm never going to find him," Sterling said under his breath.

A burst of giggling popped up beside him.

"That was fun! I suppose this isn't so bad. Is this place another realm? It's so beautiful and, wait—is it floating? Look! I can see the Pearl Castle below," Evenna said in a cheery voice, pointing with her pale ballerina-style slippers. Sterling was momentarily distracted, wondering how her shoes could be so clean after their journey so far. He gulped as he realized Evenna had caught him staring.

"These elves are crafty, hiding an entire dragon armada like this," Sterling muttered, turning his gaze back to the fields of dragons despite Evenna's pleasant chatter.

Larger than horses but smaller than other dragon breeds, their identical fur played tricks on his vision. They appeared as one huge wave of flickering sea water, another illusion.

"Um, so we have a problem. There's only one dragon that will help us, and I need your help finding him."

"What's special about one dragon? They're all so beautiful. We can befriend one. Here, let me try to conjure some oats or something," Evenna arched her deep blue eyebrow at a nearby Acreedian grazing on shrubbery and stretching its wings.

She stretched her slender hand toward the beast.

"No," Sterling scolded her. "I know you want to help, but that won't work. Acreedians only take riders they've shared a bond with. Don't let their majestic wings deceive you. They are warriors, and we don't want any reason for them to feel threatened. They are peaceful, like I promised, but they are brutal fighters if they feel threatened. My grandfather rode an Acreedian from here once. He'd be an older dragon, and he'd recognize my family blood. He'll help us if we can find him," Sterling said. He tried to mask the self-doubt that was nearly choking him, and he straightened his shoulders as he wandered to the corner of one field.

The search began, one dragon at a time. Making eye contact with a dozen or so resulted in nothing but blank stares and one boot caked in Acreedian scat.

Using sprinkles of light magic, Evenna hovered a few steps at a time (the limits of her flying power) and began to sigh.

"What's the matter?" Sterling inquired. "You know I can hear your discontent—like irritating bells ringing in my ears."

"Sorry. I just want to get this whole dragon business over with. I've sworn to stay far from winged beasts, and instead, I'm going straight into dragon kingdom."

"Why do you have to avoid dragons—other than the normal fire-breathing, flesh-eating kind of stuff?" Sterling probed as they weaved around a herd of Acreedians resting beneath a tree dripping with sparkling plumlike fruit.

"When I was very young, my caretakers told me that dragons ate witches—that they'd snatch us up and soar high into the sky to devour our flesh, spitting out witch bones as they went. I promised to never go near one."

"I can promise you that this dragon will not eat you," Sterling said with sincerity.

"Come here. Look," Sterling said as he crouched near a pile of Acreedian dung. He plucked a stick from the ground and poked the excrement, spreading it thin.

"Disgusting!"

"Yeah, but look closer," Sterling instructed as bits of fruit peels and seeds plopped around.

"They're vegetarian?" Evenna whispered with a wisp of embarrassment, turning her gaze away from Sterling.

Evenna quietly followed Sterling from field to field without further pause. Sterling's hunter vision flickered in and out, so he tried to make the best of it when it was working normally. He could scan dragons a dozen at a time with his enhanced sight, but when his hunter's blood grew tired, he relied on Evenna to help rule out the ones too small, too young, or obviously female (magenta eyes and hooves).

Amid an ordinary pasture at the base of a hill, as far as the dragon habitat reached, Sterling's neck stiffened as an Acreedian scraped its hooves against the lavender soil. It took an aggressive posture, aiming its glare at them.

Sterling stood in front of Evenna in a protective stance. He didn't want to hurt an Elvish dragon, but he wasn't sure he'd have a choice.

"I thought you said they were peaceful," she snapped.

Sterling didn't respond. It was too late. He'd already entered a standoff with the great winged beast.

CHAPTER TWENTY-EIGHT
A CONNECTION

The Acreedian lowered its head like a bull about to charge, and Sterling drew his dagger, half hoping the fiery blaze wouldn't ignite.

"Easy, buddy. I don't want any trouble," Sterling said as his blade burned with a reddish glow.

The hoofed creature's nostrils flared as he charged forward. With restored hunter reflexes, Sterling hoisted Evenna into the air, trusting her cloak to give her a gentle landing as he bolted past the dragon. His dagger tapped the sensitive spot on its hind leg, and the Acreedian beat its enormous wings together in frustration. Faster than he'd thought possible, the dragon whirled and struck Sterling's shoulder with its hoof, breaking the skin and leaving a ripe bruise. Sterling rolled and hunched into a defensive stance as the beast charged once again. As the two nearly collided, the dragon's nostrils quivered, and his head shook violently. The beast snorted loudly, the way Banefield did when he wanted his rider's attention.

"I'm not here to fight you," Sterling said, locking eyes with the creature and willing his blaze to go cold. "Go about your business." The dragon relaxed somewhat and eyed him suspiciously, but it didn't seem inclined to attack again.

All this for a ride home. Acreedians are not the majestic creatures I knew them to be, Sterling thought as he turned to leave, tucking his dagger back into its sheath.

"Sterling, look out!"

In a split second, the dragon knocked Sterling to the ground and hovered over him, sniffing Sterling's bloody shoulder like a wolf on an injured rabbit. The beast nudged Sterling, helping him to his feet before bowing to him. The dragon bent its front knee and spread one wing into the air, indicating he was ready for his riders to board.

"What's happening?" Evenna asked from the tree branch she'd been clinging to during the altercation.

"It's okay, we can ride him now. Come on down," Sterling said with a wide grin as he climbed onto the creature's back. "His fur is fluffier than horsehair. Maybe he'll let you braid it."

Sterling flashed a reassuring smile toward Evenna.

"You found the right one?"

"*We* did," Sterling replied with a boyish grin. "I

don't know what got into him, but he recognizes me now."

He helped Evenna settle in behind him and gulped when she wrapped her arms around his chest, squeezing tightly. He waited for his witch-hunter blood to react, sending ice into his core and roiling in his veins. But although his heart sped up, the sensation was almost pleasant. Somehow she smelled fresh and clean like lavender and honey. He wondered what he smelled like, then realized it was probably better not to know.

"Please take us to the village of Bren, friend."

They flew north, leaving the Pearl Castle on their swift Acreedian, and Sterling's thoughts drifted to his friends, the Story Dragon and the Red Wolf. Did they know about the dark elves? If war broke out, he desired to fight alongside them. Glancing down at his forearms, his blood pulsed without a hint of the spark he had grown used to. He missed his witch-hunter blood—like a friend he'd lost and never had a chance to properly say goodbye to.

He realized he was dozing when an unfamiliar voice in his head jarred him awake.

What kind of hunter are you?

Sterling blinked as his ears perked up, but the only sound was the wind.

"Did you hear something?" he asked Evenna.

"Shhh," she replied, loosening her grip around Sterling's chest. "It's so peaceful up here—I'm going to call this 'wind music.'"

Sterling shook his head and widened his eyes to fight the fatigue he was feeling, but as the giant dragon wings flapped, he was lulled back into a sleepy state.

How do you know the Story Dragon? The voice returned.

Sterling turned to look at Evenna. She met his gaze with a soft smile, then turned back to the clouds. Clearly, she was not hearing the voice, and he didn't think she could transform her own voice into the resonant masculine tone he was hearing.

Um, nod if you can hear me. Sterling tried wizard speak, and the dragon nodded.

I speak many languages, Sterling Fierce. Though, Elvish is my favorite. It is fate that you found me. Please accept my apologies. I sensed a connection and had mistaken you for an old enemy. What a pleasant surprise to find the kin of the brave Gregorian Fierce instead! I am called Fleggor.

"It's nice to meet you, Fleggor. Thank you for helping us," Sterling said with gratitude.

"Who are you talking to?" Evenna piped in.

"The dragon. Can't you hear him? He's using wizard speak."

"No, but I've never spoken to a dragon—probably

for the best," Evenna sulked, gripping Sterling shoulder as they swooped into a swifter air current.

Sterling adjusted the torn cloth he'd used to bandage his shoulder earlier. Although the wound was no longer bleeding, his shirt was a red-stained, tattered mess.

Sorry about the hoof slice, young Fierce.

"Don't be. You have a right to defend yourself and your home, as do all creatures of Everen. Speaking of creatures, did you say something about the Story Dragon?"

The young dragon has built a dragon fortress north of Everen and has been meeting with dragon clans to bring unity and peace among our kind. He also preaches against attacks on humans. No dragon has ever been so bold, especially in their youth. The seven sisters' power lives in his scales, ancient and wise. We are right to join his cause—he is the rightful leader of dragons, but some will resist him, naturally.

A hearty smile lit up Sterling's tanned face. He'd missed his dragon brother and was proud of his accomplishments. For a moment, flying in the wind and clouds, the complexities of dark elves and blood magic floated away, and he felt peaceful.

Evenna's head drooped to rest gently against Sterling's back. He flinched, expecting his blood to attack her. It didn't. While he was relieved his blood wasn't a threat to Evenna anymore, a hollowness festered inside him. Most of his hunter instincts had returned. He patted his prized dagger to reassure himself that he still had weapons despite losing his strongest one. He should be thankful, he reminded himself.

"Fleggor, what word is there of the Red Wolf? He is an old friend of mine, and he wasn't at his usual post guarding the Vionin Kingdom when I passed through a few days ago."

Fleggor dove beneath the clouds as the telltale circle of Lornia's Grunne stone came into view.

Evenna giggled as they plummeted in an only barely restrained freefall.

The great wolf is tracking the fog. As I must do now.

With a giant swoop, they landed at the Lornian village's doorstep.

I am sorry, young Fierce. This is where I must leave you.

Tell me how to help. I know there is a war coming, and I know about the dark elves. I want to fight, Sterling began.

"That was a wonderful ride. Thank you, Fleggor—you are the nicest dragon in Everen," Evenna said with a smile, smoothing the edge of his feathers. He nodded graciously, then turned to Sterling. The beast's wings stretched as his cream-colored eyes investigated Sterling's stormy gray ones for a fleeting moment.

Be safe, and keep the daughter of Ohann with you. She will need your protection.

"Fleggor, wait!"

A teal glow faded into the clouds along with the

sound of massive wings flapping. Then there was only silence and unanswered questions.

With the Acreedian gone, a trickle of loneliness filled the back of Sterling's throat. No matter how many times he swallowed, it seemed to always return.

CHAPTER TWENTY-NINE

TRY TO BE UNFRIENDLY

"I was wrong about dragons—at least some of them. They're much faster than traveling by horse too. No offense to Banefield..." Evenna's voice trailed off into a yawn.

Her pale arms stretched overhead as she unbraided thick strands of blue hair. Her fingers quickly knitted a new braided design, wrapped tighter and in more of a warrior style than before. She hadn't heard what Fleggor had said. But how could she? If Sterling's hunter instincts hadn't returned, he suspected he wouldn't have been able to understand an Acreedian dragon either.

Ohann and Evenna are connected somehow. Maybe the Alin will have answers about this bottle of purple death and this Ohann person, Sterling hoped.

"See, you should trust me more—especially about creatures. I am a hunter, after all," Sterling said with a boyish grin, deciding not to share what Fleggor had said.

Evenna rolled her eyes, and blue crystal colors sparkled inside them. Her energy had been restored, and for once, Sterling's stomach didn't turn cold when her power glistened.

The pair approached the Lornian village gates, which were guarded by a hooded figure the height of a child and the width of a barrel. The guard pointed lazily at them with a fighting pole.

"Greetings, my travelers. What brings you to this fine village?" A husky feminine voice growled.

"Good evening," Sterling said politely, nodding at the sun setting behind the massive stone wall that encircled the village.

"You've come to see the great Lornian wall before winter settles in to stay. The stones are impressive, aren't they?" the guard bragged as she tapped her pole against a Grunne stone.

"They're beautiful," Evenna gushed.

"It is a magnificent structure, but we're here for rest—just for the night. Then, we'll head to my home village of Bren at first light," Sterling explained.

"Bren? I'm not familiar with that village."

"We're a fishing and farming town less than a day from here. I guess we're not as well-known now that the silk trading business has slowed down," Sterling explained as a wave of fatigue washed over him. The short rest in the fairy dome and on Fleggor's back hadn't been enough to recharge his energy.

"Less than a day, eh? Why not carry on? You'd be home in your own bed by midnight if you hurried," the guard pressed. A pair of pink eyes glowed beneath the shadow of her tattered hood.

"I prefer not to travel the roads at night, and winter's approaching, so the dark comes sooner now. And these aren't the safest times," Sterling whispered with a wink, patting his bloody shoulder.

The guard nodded then tilted her head at Evenna, who was pressing her face against one of the giant Grunne stones. "What's her story, hunter?"

"Uh, her mind is still young," he admitted, instantly regretting his lack of disguise for Evenna. While he was in obvious hunter garb, she was in a cloak that could've passed for Elvish.

Wait, that's it!

"...as a human raised by elves, she's taking some time to acclimate to our ways," he clarified with a confident smile. There was no way he was about to admit that he had a witch in his company, especially one powerful enough to destroy the entire village—if she wanted to.

The guard used her fighting pole to lift the hem of Evenna's cloak. She raised it to eye level and rubbed the velvety material in between her greasy, plump fingers.

"I haven't felt an Elvish robe in some time. They are as lush and pure as ever," the guard sighed, obviously disappointed to have no further questions. "You both may enter Lornia for one night."

Sterling nodded, and Evenna performed an awkward curtsy.

"Boys, we have a princess in our midst," the guard giggled, and several other guards revealed themselves along the narrow walkway on top of the stone walls. She unlatched the stone door and whispered an enchantment. Stone ground against stone, sliding just far enough that only one person could pass at a time. Sterling took Evenna's hand and gestured for her to go first. The guard bounced high into the air with her pole, pouncing over Sterling's head, and landing softly on a hanging lamp. Her child-size body flipped upside down, which placed her face exactly even with Sterling's and close enough that he could detect the temperature of her breath.

"You have much to teach her," the guard said in a low whisper before releasing a spine-tingling cackle.

The disturbing laughter echoed against the stone until at last the stone door closed with a grand thump behind them.

Two more guards melted into the shadows as Sterling left the shelter of the doorway. Had Sterling's hunter vision not returned, the gray guards would've been undetectable.

"Lornians sure are odd," Evenna retorted with a naive smile.

She traced her slippers over the river rock path that wound in a spiral toward the village center.

"Those aren't the usual Lornian guards. The trained warriors are likely preparing for war, so they hired mercenaries to guard the door—brutal troops but hardly loyal. With the dark elves in the castle—" Sterling bit off his next words, and he scolded himself for jumping to conclusions. He couldn't assume what he'd seen in the elven city was as bad as it looked after only a fleeting glance. His stomach groaned, offering the perfect distraction. "C'mon, let's get dinner," he suggested as Evenna chewed her lower lip. It had to be hard to hear about the chaos in the world when she'd only just been set free to experience it.

Moments later, they sat at a handmade table carved from honeywood in a crowded tavern. Folks of every race were stuffed around tables, many of them shooting each other suspicious glances. The place was filled with nervous tension, and Sterling gulped as he realized it wouldn't take much to set the whole thing off.

He stared at the whorled pattern of the wood in front of him and tried to ignore the jostling of tavern-goers shifting and gesticulating behind him. His stomach had begun to knot as soon as they'd entered the village—and it wasn't just hunger. He sensed dark energy lurking nearby. Sterling's blood pulsed warmer as his mind reeled with images of desolate villages and war-torn remains smudged in purple char—and shadow soldiers marching to the dark elves' orders.

Suddenly, Evenna's elbow struck his ribs, and he released the glass bottle in his pocket that he hadn't realized he'd grasped.

"Hey!" Sterling said as he shot a scolding glance at Evenna. She gestured impatiently to a dark-haired woman with a tired expression.

"I ask only twice for an order—after that, you'd have to track me down. What'll it be, hon?" she asked, shifting her overflowing tray of ale mugs.

"Sorry—long day of traveling. I'll have anything with meat in it. Thanks," Sterling said, eying the taverngoers.

The waitress turned on her heels to clomp to her next table. Meanwhile, Evenna's eyes lit up.

"This place is so lively! The smells and sounds— the different kinds of people. I've never been anywhere like this," she gushed, smiling at the taverngoers at the next table.

It was true. The tiny space was crawling with nonlocals, which wasn't at all typical this time of year. This should have been the season for scraping together the last harvests in preparation for winter and planting any cold-weather seedlings while the ground was soft enough to take them. These must be people trying to stay out of potential combat zones or looking for work as guards, but the whole place made Sterling uneasy. If he hadn't needed food and rest, he'd have left already.

"I know it's exciting, but we have to keep a low profile. This human-raised-by-elves story is skimpy at best. Look, Evenna, out here we must keep our heads down. For all we know, that guard-for-hire tipped off your elders. Someone could be on their way to find you right now. Can you please try *not to* get noticed? Pretend you are dull and boring, that you aren't interested in anyone but yourself," Sterling begged, stuffing a handful of tavern corn chips into his mouth.

"This is my first time feeling alive—free—my first time to feel like a normal girl. I've never had a chance to make friends with folks or even talk to anyone outside my coven. And now you want me to be unfriendly?" she gasped.

Sterling nodded in the somber way his father would when the truth was too hard to explain with words.

"Please, just until I can be sure you're somewhere safe."

"Fine. I'll just be like you. Quiet. Boring. Unfriendly," she scoffed.

But it was too late. A water sprite had locked eyes with Evenna and was weaving its liquid mass through the crowd straight toward their table.

CHAPTER THIRTY
THE WATER SPRITES' LURE

Sterling didn't have time to warn Evenna about water sprites and how they tempted living beings into their streams, lakes, and rivers. It wouldn't have been all that threatening except that water sprites tended to keep their land-dwelling companions underwater longer than they should—a fatal consequence.

"You seek friendship with the waters," the sprite announced.

Sterling swiped a corn chip onto the floor, ducking beneath the table and pretending to pick it up. He needed a moment to gather his thoughts, and his instincts told him to avoid eye contact with the watery beings. Under the table, he studied the translucent human-shaped figure. Instead of legs, it stood on a gentle waterspout. An overwhelming urge came over him to touch the swirling, liquid-like skin. He imagined how smooth and cool the water would feel. Suddenly, his outstretched fingers snapped back as if commanded by another force. His veins pulsed with a familiar warmth before settling back down.

My blood magic? He wondered if some of it had escaped the curse and returned to him—could it be possible?

With a hefty sigh of confusion, he stared at the worn-out wooden floorboards and wished the water sprite would melt into a puddle and seep beneath them. He'd come so close to delivering Evenna to safety and refused to let another problem stop him from finishing his quest.

But Evenna was engaged in full conversation with the water sprite. Though her words were muffled at first, there was no mistaking her chipper tone. She sounded so different from the shy, suspicious witch he'd met in the tree hollow. He didn't like it. Her words rang through the tavern's hum of casual conversation.

"Oh, I love your color! You're like a slippery water globe—but you're alive!"

Sterling held his breath, saying every hunter prayer he knew, hoping that the sprite would lose interest and leave them alone.

"We should spend time together if your friend doesn't mind," the water sprite suggested.

"We don't mind if you come with us to Bren—it's a small fishing village less than a day's ride! That's where we're heading. Right, Sterling?!"

Then, something clicked.

She's been enchanted, he realized.

As suspected, making eye contact with a sprite was a mistake, but he didn't want the strange creatures to know that he knew that. Sterling popped his head up, rubbing his eyes and taking note of a second water sprite approaching.

"Everen's stars, these chips are salty! Got a grain of it in my eye. Come with me, Evenna—help me get to our horse. Please excuse us now."

He risked a shifty glance at Evenna. She'd let her hood down, revealing her gentle features in the glow of the tavern lights. Her face was screwed up in a pout, and her eyes swirled, glassy and blue.

"But we don't have a horse," she started.

I'm going to regret not eating a decent meal, he decided as he planned the fastest path to an exit.

Before Evenna could finish her sentence, Sterling tossed a handful of ale mugs strategically across the tavern. They crashed, and the crowd fractured as different races turned against each other, assuming a fight had been initiated. Soon, the tavern was filled with insults and punches. The shouting unified into a deafening roar, and the two water sprites were buried in the chaos.

Sterling looped his arm around Evenna's waist and carried her under his arm as he ducked toward the exit. No one heard her protests over the roar of the crowd, but she fought him each step of the way. He was almost at the exit when he felt her slender body slip out of her cloak. He turned to grab her, but she had slipped through a gap much smaller than she should have been able to fit through. With no other option, he plunged back into the crowd, finally catching up to her as she passed the tavern owner. He had burst from the kitchen and was rapidly seizing brawlers and forcing them to the floor.

Evenna shrieked as Sterling wrapped his arm around her once more.

"Stop fighting. You'll only get twisted up, and then it'll really hurt. I'm not trying to fight you!" he said through gritted teeth.

Begrudgingly he maneuvered his biceps and placed Evenna in a hunter's hold.

"Ow! You're hurting me! Let me stay with the waters!" Evenna squealed.

"You leave me no choice—Evenna, you're enchanted. I've got to get you out of here before the whole place knows you're here. It's bad enough you told the sprites where we were going," he whispered, carefully eyeing the tavern's far corner. There was a camouflaged door meant only for tavern staff—their best chance to escape.

Taverngoers paid no attention to the quarreling pair slipping toward the back door in a mix of flying elbows and smashed chairs. But two sets of eyes, stoic and liquid, burned through Sterling like lasers. He knew they would come for Evenna—if not now, then later. Water sprites never stopped hunting their prey, and like whispers in the wind, they were ever-present in nature. This was bad, but Sterling was sure the Alin would know what to do—if they could just get home.

Once outside the tavern, Sterling untangled Evenna and hoped that the night air would restore her mind. As with many enchantments, changing environments was enough to weaken it.

"What are we doing out here?" she asked as if she had forgotten the whole event. Sterling groaned, and his stomach pitched in with a sad gurgle. He pulled Evenna's cloak out of the crook of his arm and swept the fabric over her, concealing her glossy hair once more. He scanned the area for the nearest stable.

"We must leave. It's not safe here now that you've been noticed. Evenna, there are creatures and wizards and who knows what else tracking you. They will stop at nothing to harm you or return you to your elders. You gotta snap out of this."

"The waters could keep me safe," she whispered.

"You're enchanted, Evenna. It's going to take time to wear off, but you have to come with me now. I made a promise to your grandfather. And I can't protect you like this," he explained.

Evenna kept quiet, either too confused or bewildered to respond. But she didn't flee—she followed Sterling to the horse stalls. Sterling hummed an old hunter bedtime tune as he untied a stallion with a coat as black as night. He cupped two handfuls of oats from a nearby feed satchel and spoke to the horse like an old friend. The horse was massive, taller, and wider than Banefield. Whoever rode him was likely also large. Sterling shuddered, hoping the giant mystery rider was deep inside the tavern scuffle, weighed down by one too many ales.

"If we want to make it to Bren as fast as possible, we have to borrow this horse," he said in a serious tone that could have passed for his father's.

Sterling motioned for her to step into the stirrup, unsure if she'd comply or turn and run back inside the tavern and to the water sprites.

"So now we're stealing horses?" she huffed, stepping on Sterling's toe, then leveraging herself against his knee to reach the stirrup.

"No," he replied.

Sterling scratched the scraggly hair hiding behind his fuller auburn beard and plucked a corn chip out of it. He chomped loudly with his mouth open as he climbed into the saddle and wrapped his arms around her, nabbing the reins.

"We're stealing *a* horse."

The Lornian gate guard had changed, this time a gentle-looking older fellow that didn't notice a second rider hidden beneath Sterling's cape. In the darkness, their disguise of one large heap of a rider worked. The horse seemed well-rested and familiar with navigating the dirt path west of town. They traveled with fresh night air against their faces, and Sterling frequently squeezed his heels into the horse's sides to keep the stallion charging at top speed. If they had to travel during a moonless night, they'd better travel fast. Whatever lurked about at this hour, with any luck, would be too surprised by the speeding mass to attack them. It wasn't the best plan, but it was all he had.

It wasn't long before the trotting rocked Evenna to sleep. Minutes bled into hours. Sterling, too, felt comforted by the lull of the ride and the familiar wafts of wheat fields and horse sweat swimming in his nose. Judging by the blackness of the sky, it was the dead of night. They were halfway to Bren, according to Sterling's rough calculations. It was difficult to be sure without sunlight, but there was a glint of sparkles mixed into the dirt path to keep them on the well-worn West Road. The landscape of dark wheat fields whooshed in the breeze, and a pitch-dark horizon stretched out to a beautiful emptiness.

Out of the darkness, rusting stirred, and wheat crops snapped.

Sterling's hunter hearing detected it in the distance at first, a handful of fields away, and he hoped it would keep its distance. But soon, the crunching of wheat stalks told him it drew close, and it was immensely weighty.

The hobbelston. Sterling recalled the Alin's night-time monster and kicked himself for letting it slip his mind.

The stallion's ears twitched toward the sound, and horse hooves slowed.

"Yes, something is out there, buddy. Keep alert and be ready to go as fast or hide. I won't let you get hurt," Sterling whispered to the horse, patting his sweaty neck.

Out of a sea of wheat, a beast the size of a house emerged. The horse balked and took a few steps back as the monster oozed onto the path only a few steps in front of them. Taking advantage of his restored hunter vision, Sterling made out its general shape, a lopsided clump with thick slime dripping from an open hole in its center. As the hole widened, rows of gnarled teeth made their appearance. Sterling drew his dagger and pointed it toward the beast, the blade crackling with red dragon fire.

The beast unleashed a pale gray tongue, covered in bumps. As it flopped toward Sterling, it split into two smaller whiplike extremities, thorned and remarkably nimble. One gooey whip slung toward him, undeterred by the flaming blade, and wrapped around his other hand. Sterling tried to slice it, but the blade only grazed the slippery whip.

"Sterling!" Evenna screamed. The horse shrieked as well, trying to bolt, but between the monster's tongue and Sterling's firm grip on the saddle, it was stuck. It thrashed and kicked, but it couldn't dislodge the second whiplike tongue that had seized Evenna.

Then she was gone, dangling in the air over the beast's gaping maw.

"Wait!" Sterling called, and the monster twitched its one giant yellow eyeball toward him.

Evenna's fingertips glowed, ready to burst with light magic at the foul beast. Her chest heaved, and for a moment, the pair locked eyes and his body experienced a familiar statue-like feeling.

Evenna had stopped time, but it wouldn't last. She was too panicked to stay focused for long.

Evenna, it wants your grandfather—you by extension—not me. We can trick it. Send your magic to my blade—I'll get you out. Hunter's promise, Sterling said in his mind.

Evenna shut her eyes as time unfroze and the beast swung her body headfirst into its quivering mouth. A beam of light escaped her fingertips just before she was enveloped. Sterling's dagger crackled with white sparks and mist, the white flames twisting with the red dragon flame. A shriek pierced the night as the fiery blade slashed through the monster's roped tongue, freeing Sterling from its grasp. It didn't have a chance to react as the witch hunter stood and leaped from his horse toward it. Sterling stabbed and hacked at its gelatinous skin until its giant eyeball drooped. Using all his hunter strength, Sterling cut the monster in half and pulled Evenna to safety.

"Are you okay?!" Sterling shouted over a high-pitched sound he assumed came from the monster.

Drenched in snot-like goo but otherwise unharmed, Evenna's eyes shot open.

"Cape," she demanded, grabbing Sterling's cape. She wiped her eyes, nose, and mouth.

Sterling surveyed the night sky, less dark than

before, then realized the screaming noise was coming from his own dagger.

A warning.

"Move!"

He rolled them both as far away from the monster's corpse as he could manage before a glowing sphere sprang from the goop and barreled toward them. Reflexively, Sterling threw his dagger. It split the sphere, shattering it. A yolk-like substance oozed from its lone eye, and Sterling decided he wouldn't eat eggs again for a very long time. The house-sized ball of slime vibrated, then shriveled into thousands of tiny, black worms writhing toward the nearby wheat crops before vanishing from sight. The pieces would, in time, reform into another monster, angrier than the last. But for the time being, it was defeated.

"Well, that's gross," Evenna admitted, smiling at Sterling, and rubbing the dagger-shaped scar on her neck that had mysteriously grown more pronounced.

CHAPTER THIRTY-ONE
THERE'S NO PLACE LIKE HOME

Sterling was grateful that the stallion they'd aggressively borrowed had obviously been through a few fights. Although it had fled during the battle, he and Evenna had found it peacefully grazing in the shelter of a small patch of clover just around the bend. The horse was understandably hesitant to return to the scene of the fight, and as soon as they passed the splatters of muck, the horse leaped into a full gallop that Sterling could barely control.

As the sun rose, Sterling and Evenna breached the Bren border and finally convinced the sweaty horse to slow to a walk. Winding up the road to the Alin's cottage had never felt so good.

They were greeted by a jealous snort as Banefield limped from the pasture. Sterling dismounted and collapsed into a hug around Banefield's neck. The herbal-scented bandages sent a lump into his throat.

Despite overcoming a myriad of dangers, Sterling's success had come at a price.

"I missed you too, buddy," Sterling said sweetly as he stroked his faithful horse's neck.

Evenna wasted no time giving Banefield a two-handed nose scratch while Sterling led the black stallion to a water trough and removed its saddle.

"We should return the horse to Lornia when things calm down," Sterling said.

"I fear the roads may not be safe for travel for some time," a voice inside the cottage insisted.

"He's home!" Evenna squealed. Despite the dangers outside of Bren, she was happy. For now, she was safe—and she was home.

Sterling and Evenna shared a smile and rushed to the Alin's porch. The door creaked open by itself, welcoming them inside. Whiffs of peppercorn and creamy chicken soup permeated the air, and a cross breeze caressed floor-length curtains with stitched-in silk flowers.

"Where is he?" Evenna whispered, squirming in her slippers.

Sterling squinted at the kitchen and grinned, pointing at the tip of the Alin's pointed hood. An invisibility spell flickered over the old man, but his form finally emerged. Evenna squeezed her fists, obviously trying to hold back tears as the Alin's long gray beard appeared over his star-and-moon robe.

"You really outdid yourself, Tomorak!" Sterling

remarked, spying a half dozen loaves of freshly baked rosemary bread.

Evenna ran, clutching her grandfather in a loving hug. Next to him, she looked even more delicate than before.

"Granda, I was worried I'd never see you again!" she said with a sniffle.

"Ah, my dear. I made a promise that I would always keep you safe. Did my hunter look after you?" he queried, eying Sterling, who'd helped himself to a mouthful of rosemary bread.

"Myeah, mut mit mustn't measy," he garbled, stuffing another chunk of fresh-baked bread in his mouth.

Evenna shot a pouty face at Sterling, but her eyes twinkled. "Well, all things considered, he managed to deliver me to you. And he kept me safe," she confessed, her cheeks aglow.

Just then, the cottage door shivered with a hefty knock. The enchanted entrance flung itself open, and Uncle Roag barreled through.

"Right on time, Nephew! It's good to see you safe and sound. My messenger beetles told me the night-shade butterflies saw a witch hunter in Lornia. I came straight away. I bottled a jar of watermelon juice, my secret recipe, to celebrate the occasion!" He held up a sticky flask.

Uncle Roag's robust laughter, sparkling green eyes, and food-stained clothing meant that Sterling was finally home.

"You got more crumbs in your beard than all the kitchens in the kingdom, Uncle," Sterling remarked. He pointed to a few new gray strands in his uncle's beard. "Oh look, more of those mouse tails are growin' in!"

Uncle Roag gave him a sturdy shoulder pat, then seemed to change his mind and squeezed Sterling into a ferocious hug accompanied by a brutal head rub until they both collapsed with laughter.

"I like him already," Evenna interjected.

Uncle Roag's eyes darted toward the slender, pale young lady tucked away in the corner.

"And who might you be? Our young light witch, I presume?"

Evenna gave the same awkward curtsy she'd given the Lornian guard.

"My name is Evenna, granddaughter of Tomorak, the world-famous Alin," she gushed, squeezing her grandfather in a hug and nearly disappearing in the thick, velvety creases of his celestial-patterned robe.

"It's awfully good to meet ya. I'm Roag Burdbee, Sterling's favorite uncle. My, she's a beauty, Sterling! Not such a terrible quest after all, huh?" Uncle Roag said, winking and jabbing Sterling with his meaty elbow. Sterling studiously avoided meeting Evenna's eye as a blush threatened to creep up his neck. He turned to the Alin.

"Speaking of my quest, I have news." Sterling's good humor disappeared, and he tried to swallow the lump that had appeared in his throat.

"Go on," Uncle Roag said as the grin left his face.

"We found something in the elven castle—buried away in a secret storage room. It's the source of the fog—dark elven magic. One got loose—a dark elf soldier. It nearly killed me. It would've if it hadn't been for Evenna's magic," Sterling said, handing the bottle to the Alin. Tomorak held it up to the light, watching the thick purple smoke swirl.

"And don't forget about the water sprites and the monster roaming around Bren," Evenna reminded him.

"You've met my hobbelston?" the Alin inquired, relighting his pipe with the glowing orange tip of his wand. "Did he have one eye or has a second grown in yet? Troublesome monster won't leave me alone."

Evenna snickered.

"He won't bother you for a while, anyway," Sterling said reassuringly.

"That is most helpful," the Alin said as he puffed a ring of pipe smoke around the glass bottle in his palm.

"Sir, um, with all respect, can you please lock that bottle away? After what the last one did—" Sterling stopped suddenly, tilting his ear to the forest. His veins throbbed.

Evenna sat up straight, rubbing her dagger scar.

"What do you hear, Sterling?" she asked. He was distracted for a second, realizing how good she'd gotten at reading his moods. Then the sound came again.

Sterling bolted from the Alin's cottage and

unsheathed his dagger, revealing a bright red fire with distinct white sparks twirling at the ends. The world seemed to grow quiet, waiting for Sterling's next move. At the tip of his blade, a small, winged creature froze, eyes wide.

The Alin clapped, breaking the stillness.

"My, my, what a show! Sterling, you can put away your weapon. I'm quite sure Premadora means us no real harm."

"It takes more than a fancy beard and firework blade to impress me!" Premadora teased, shaking off her surprise.

Sterling tucked his dagger away and self-consciously ran his fingers over his spots of facial hair. Even patchy and fine, it felt like a miniature version of his father's and uncle's beards.

He laughed and held out his hand so Premadora could land on his palm. "Surely the sparkling blade is at least a little impressive."

"Nothing is as sparkly as me," she said saucily, shaking glittering fairy dust over his fingers.

That evening beneath the stars, Sterling, Evenna, the Alin, Uncle Roag, and Premadora huddled around an enchanted, purple-flamed campfire. They chuckled about Banefield's heroic distraction as a unicorn and how foolish the elders must have felt after realizing their mistake. Evenna spoke of the donkey wizard's illusions and the carnivorous sludge in the depths of the Swamplands. Sterling described his transformation into a snake, the Elvish guard's intuition, and Queen Clarelle's unparalleled healing magic. Long after the others drifted to sleep, Sterling and Premadora watched the fiery embers smolder, letting off lavender smoke that spiraled into the starlit sky above.

"You know a war has begun, Sterling. The dark elves grow in number, and it's only a matter of time before they attack our village—they will attack us all. No one and nowhere will be safe. Destiny brought you and the light witch together—and now your blade glows with both red and white flames—your powers are stronger together, and I suspect you both will fight the dark elves when the time comes. You will need to keep your friends, new and old, as close as you can," Premadora lectured as gently as a plendi could.

"Yes, Premadora. Every instinct I have tells me so," Sterling replied. His veins thrummed as if in agreement, and he relaxed into the familiar warmth. His blood magic had returned, but he would not harm Evenna—not because of any quest or loyalty to the Alin, but because he was ready to, and he was in control now.

A LOOK AT BOOK THREE:
STERLING FIERCE AND THE BATTLE OF THE ELVES

Embark on a gripping journey with Sterling as he faces bewildering magical forces and tests the bonds of friendship in the epic conclusion of the *Sterling Fierce* trilogy.

When a powerful light witch, Evenna, vanishes under mysterious circumstances, Sterling is propelled into a desperate search across unknown realms. With the looming war of the elves threatening everything he holds dear, Sterling vows to find Evenna at any cost.

As Sterling delves deeper into the secrets of elemental magic and the enigma behind Evenna's disappearance, he must forge unlikely alliances to overcome daunting challenges. But with limited abilities and a deadly toxin coursing through his blood, Sterling realizes he cannot win this battle alone.

Only by embracing the courage to trust in others and becoming a true pack leader can Sterling hope to navigate the treacherous path ahead and safeguard those he cares about. Will he harness the skills of his allies to unravel the mystery and emerge victorious, or will darkness prevail?

AVAILABLE APRIL 2024

ACKNOWLEDGMENTS

I am forever grateful to Wise Wolf Books and each editor I have had the pleasure of working with over the years. I owe a great deal to my mentor, David, and sincerely appreciate the support of friends and family from near and far.

Thank you, once again, to my husband for tolerating my evening hours spent away, adventuring in Everen. To my boys, Brenner and Bryce, thank you for going on this journey with me.

ABOUT THE AUTHOR

Lori Tchen was born and raised in the Texas hill country where shaking out one's shoes for scorpions was part of the daily norm. She writes fiction in the evenings, her highly prized downtime outside of work, while raising her two sons.

Lori's career began in criminology, working deep nights in a detention facility, then investigating crimes as a Texas State Enforcement Agent. After observing the underbelly of society, her fantasy stories allow her and her readers to escape into imagined worlds and inspire bravery in children (and adults alike) to face some of life's evil characters.